Be My Valentine

R.J. Groves

16pt

Copyright Page from the Original Book

Title: BE MY VALENTINE

Copyright © 2021 by R. J. Groves

Published by
Escape
An imprint of Harlequin Enterprises (Australia) Pty Limited (ABN 47 001 180 918), a subsidiary of HarperCollins Publishers Australia Pty Limited (ABN 36 009 913 517)
Level 13, 201 Elizabeth St
SYDNEY NSW 2000
AUSTRALIA

www.romance.com.au

TABLE OF CONTENTS

i

Be My Valentine
R.J. Groves

A seamstress. A naval officer. An impossible decision.

Harley Smith has always been unlucky in love, and this year is no different. Even if she can't get her best friend's brother out of her head. It's been almost a year, and with Valentine's Day approaching and no date in sight, perhaps it's time to stop holding out hope on her dreams. Maybe she should make her own happily ever after...

Joey Gray is a sailor through and through. He's been hurt before, and his job has become the only thing he can truly count on. But then he met his sister's best friend—the woman who has filled his dreams for months on end, regardless of how much he has tried to forget her. Now his career isn't as fulfilling as it once was, and he knows who's responsible. He needs to see her again. And what better day to tell her how he feels than on her birthday—Valentine's Day?

But is one week enough time to figure out what they have?

About R.J. Groves

Australian author R.J. Groves has been passionate about writing since she could put pen to paper and can usually be found jotting plots and stories down on anything she can get her hands on. Describing herself as a mum, wife, author, and coffee lover, her other passions include music, cooking, books, adventures, and searching for plot bunnies in even the most mundane activities.

Facebook: www.facebook.com/rjgauthor

Twitter: www.twitter.com/rjg_author

Instagram: www.instagram.com/r.j.groves_author

Mailing list: http://eepurl.com/dArMXf

Website: www.rjgrovesauthor.com

Acknowledgements

To my Tribe, the writing friends I've made along the way who are always there to motivate and encourage. To my Escape family for all the behind-the-scenes work you do in getting each story out there. You're all amazing! To my readers for your kind words and for taking the time to read my books and follow my journey—thank you! To my incredible family, my biggest supporters and soundboards. I couldn't do any of this without you.

To Mike.

Chapter 1

'You're leaving us, Gray?'

Joey glanced over at his best friend, Ryan Burgin, as he held his push-up in the high position to catch his breath. 'What gives you that impression?'

Ryan pressed out a few more push-ups before rolling onto his back for some crunches. 'Rumour has it you've already had your second lot of leave approved in how many months?'

Joey flipped onto his back and joined his friend with crunches of his own. 'Not seeing your point, Burgin.'

Ryan pulled himself to a sitting position, hooking his arms around his knees. 'Ten years in the navy and you've rarely taken personal leave. Twice in a year is gonna raise some eyebrows.'

'Don't see how it's anyone's business.'

'Word spreads easily when you're living with confinements. Who died?'

Joey could feel the tightening of his muscles as he moved. Though still early in the day, the heat of the summer sun bore down on him, intensifying the warmth spreading through his body from the workout. He loved working on the sea, on the HMAS *Mallee,* floating around with nothing but blue water and marine life around him and the crew. He was born to be a sailor and he wouldn't trade it for the world, even if some things were less than ideal. Like the inability to truly escape the harshness of the sun and the occasional lack of reception preventing him from being able to reach the people on land he cared about. Or one person, in particular.

It felt like an age since he'd seen Harley. Oh, the way her hazel eyes lit up at his corny jokes and stories. The way her laughter tore through his whole body, making him feel like his mission was to keep that smile on her face for as long as he lived. And he'd found that he could be himself around her.

For the first time in his life as a sailor, he hadn't wanted to get back on the ship.

Sure, nothing had *happened,* per se. He'd met her when she was crying on his sister's couch after a bad breakup for Pete's sake. And contrary to popular belief, he wasn't the kind of guy to jump a vulnerable woman. Nor was he the kind of guy to just sleep with any willing woman. But where were the stories in that? His fellow seamen thrived on his stories and he was certain no one really cared about the validity of them.

Stories were what kept the ship going—what kept every cog of this well-oiled machine running smoothly. Ryan was the only person who knew the bulk of his stories were full of it, but he'd also never turned down an opportunity to hear one. Joey fell back against the deck of the ship, covering his face with his hands to block out the sun.

'No one died,' he said, realising he hadn't answered Ryan's question. 'Just got leave built up, so I may as well use some.'

'Anything to do with that girl you left behind?'

'So what if it is?'

Ryan shook his head, his expression amused, then moved to prop himself up on his toes and elbows in a plank while Joey followed suit. 'You sure nothing happened last time you were on leave?'

Joey held the plank, feeling the burn until his whole body felt like it was beginning to shake. 'Harley's a friend.'

Ryan snorted. 'Friend, my ass. Don't think I haven't noticed how often you check your phone.'

'You stalking me, Burgin?' Joey teased.

'Hard not to notice when you never used to carry it around and now it's a fifth appendage.'

Joey laughed. Ryan had a point. He'd never been attached to his phone. What was the point when the chances of getting reception out here were so slim? But since he'd come back from visiting his sister, Andie, in Perth, he couldn't help but hope that he just might stumble across a bar or two of reception and have a message come in from the lovely brunette he couldn't get out of his head. For a while, he'd managed to message Harley each day, made the occasional call too. But lately? Nada.

'You know how it is, mate,' Ryan continued, suddenly growing serious. 'Guy finds a girl, falls in love and shit, then she decides she's not cut out to be a sailor's wife.'

Joey sucked in a shaky breath of air, glancing sideways at Ryan. He knew Ryan was speaking from experience and he felt for him—he did. But Harley was different. He couldn't tell how, but he just ... knew. There was something about her that he just couldn't push aside. Something he wanted—needed—to explore.

'Harley's a friend.' *But I'm hoping to change that.* Joey pushed himself up to his feet and Ryan did the same, puffing. 'C'mon. Race ya.'

***

'Set a date, yet?' Harley asked, walking beside her auburn-haired best friend.

Andie scoffed. 'We'd need a ring first.'

'Do you think Tay's far off it?'

Harley folded her arms across her chest, the evening breeze cool despite the hot days of late. She had to admit, she was a little jealous of her friend. She'd somehow managed to find a stand-up guy following her broken engagement. Andie and Tay were perfect for each other. It was only a matter of time before he popped the question. Her thoughts drifted to her own love life—or *lack thereof.* For a while she'd been messaging back and forth with the handsome dark-haired man who'd made her smile again after she'd broken things off with Angelo. Harley made a mental note to never get involved with a neighbour again. Or anyone in her building of units, for that matter.

Joey had brought a smile to her face when she'd thought it was impossible. He'd made her laugh when her heart had been breaking. He'd shown her that good guys actually do exist. He'd made her hope again.

And he also happened to be Andie's younger brother and spent a lot of time on the sea. At least Andie and Tay both lived in Perth. She'd barely heard from Joey the last few months. She sighed, bringing her focus back to her friend just in time to catch the end of what Andie was saying.

'I think I'd be ready for it.'

'Ready for what?'

Andie shot a look towards her, her brows pulled together. 'To say yes. If Tay proposed.'

'Babe, you were born ready,' Harley said, trying to pull herself from her pity party and get in the right mood for the evening.

'What about you? Heard from Joey?' Andie asked, stretching an arm high to wave to the woman ahead, the rich blonde hair unmistakeable. Libby—Tay's sister—waved back excitedly and started towards them.

'Um, no,' Harley muttered, picking up the pace to catch up with Libby. 'I don't think that's—no.'

Andie frowned at her, but they caught up with Libby before she could say anything more. Harley let out a breath, relieved she wouldn't have to go into detail before a girls' night out. Especially since this was supposed to be about her. Libby shrieked as she pulled her and Andie into a group hug and pulled back with a little dance.

'Ready to party, gorgeous humans?' Libby said. She looked more like an excited child than a grown woman about to have a few drinks with her friends.

Andie laughed. 'Well, married life certainly hasn't slowed you down, has it, Lib?'

'Does Connor really know what he's got himself into?' Harley teased, glad to have Libby's energy around. It was hard to be down in the dumps with Libby in tow. It was only after her and Connor's wedding that Harley really became friends with Libby—thanks to Andie.

Libby giggled, putting her smaller form between Harley and Andie and looping her arms through theirs. 'If he hasn't worked it out by now, I'm not sure he ever will. But we're not here to talk about me.' Libby swayed her hips so she bumped into Harley. 'We're here for you! Even if we're celebrating a day early. Seriously, having a birthday on *Valentine's Day?* Oh, the romance.'

Before she could stop herself, Harley made a sound that was somewhere between a choked laugh and a snort. Romance, indeed. That was the last thing on her mind right now. Especially since there really wasn't a man in sight to cater to such romance.

Her stomach twisted as she thought of Joey again. She didn't understand. She'd thought they had something. She'd even gone so far as to practically admit to Andie that things were serious. Well, at least she'd thought they had been. Joey had only been gone a month when she'd said that, and they'd been messaging and talking to each other on the phone a lot of that time. She'd blushed every time she saw his name pop up on the screen. Her heart had pounded in her chest and her stomach had filled with butterflies when she'd heard his voice, his laugh, trailing through the phone. She'd thought he must have felt the same way—why else would he have wanted to talk to her so much?

Clearly, she was wrong. Because after that first month, the calls gradually became less frequent, the messages more sparse, and the doubts settled in. Had she fallen for the wrong guy again? Had she read the signs all wrong and thought there was something there that wasn't? To put it simply, she'd felt like she'd been friend-zoned. And possibly not even that. Hell, he'd probably forgotten all about her by now.

'But really,' Libby continued. Harley blinked back to the present, realising that Libby hadn't stopped talking that whole time. 'We *could* have celebrated tomorrow. Just because it's Valentine's Day doesn't mean we can't party on Harley's birthday, right?'

Libby and Andie both turned their focus on her. Harley swallowed. 'Oh, no, we couldn't. Come on, this is your first Valentine's as a married woman, and Andie's first Valentine's with Tay. I wouldn't want to take that away from you guys. Besides, the night before is perfectly fine. Neither the food nor the drinks will have that surcharge added to it.'

But if Harley was being honest with herself, it wasn't the fact it was Andie and Libby's first Valentine's with their other halves that made her not want to celebrate on her birthday. She just simply never did Valentine's. For starters, she'd never been with a guy at that time of the year—somehow, her relationships had all ended before the season, or started well after it. She was the kind of girl who guys lost interest in quickly. She knew her looks were pretty average and she probably could lose a few kilos. Or ten. And to be honest, she probably wasn't even that exciting. But she didn't care. She was more than happy to curl up with a blanket on the couch and read the night away.

Or, at least, she used to be. Until Joey. Since she'd met Joey, the couch didn't seem to have quite the same appeal as it used to. But that had to stop. He clearly wasn't interested in her.

Story of her life.

Sure, she'd always dreamed of her own happily ever after—who didn't? But she was also realistic. And the reality of the matter was that she always fell for the wrong guys—hard and fast—and she always ended up hurt. Maybe she was destined to be alone. She should just keep on being happy for her friends and focus on helping all the lucky brides who come into her work to find their perfect wedding gown.

And it was with that thought in mind that she went into the classy bar with the girls and allowed herself to have a few drinks too many. By the end of the night, she felt free and relaxed. She was strong and independent and didn't need a guy to make her happy. She was Harley Smith, and she could take on the world with all twenty-nine years of experience she had.

Screw any guy who wanted to mess with her feelings!

Screw Joey!

Chapter 2

Harley groaned as she slowly came to her senses, her extremely vivid dream still niggling at her mind. Screw Joey, indeed. She rolled over and regretted it instantly, her stomach churning and her head spinning. And there was a loud, irritating noise piercing her brain. She squinted through heavy eyelids and patted around on her bed until she found the source of the noise and answered it with a grunt.

'Happy birthday!' The excited voice on the other end of the line only made her head throb more.

'Libby, how are you still functioning?' she mumbled into the phone.

Libby giggled. 'Oh, honey, for starters, you had at least twice as much to drink as I did. And I've already had breakfast, done my morning yoga and had my green tea.'

Harley groaned again, the thought of twisting her body into any position except her current one making her stomach lurch more. *And* green tea?

Ugh. Just the mention of food had her stomach churning.

'I hate you.'

Libby laughed again and Harley might have said more had her body not threatened to bring up her insides if she dared open her mouth again. 'Love you, too, Harley. Now, have a shower and find yourself some coffee. You'll feel better for it.'

Harley hung up the phone, finally forcing her eyes open enough to look down her body. She'd somehow ended up with a blanket on, but she was still wearing the same clothes from the night before. With another grunt, she rolled over and went back to sleep.

***

It was close to noon when Harley finally managed to tear herself away from her bed. Her shower was welcoming, the hot water washing away the remnants of the night before and soothing her head. She'd caught a glimpse of herself in the mirror while drying off and found herself staring at her reflection longer than she normally would.

Was she any different now that she was a year older? At twenty-eight, she'd thought she had the world at her feet—that time was on her side. There had still been plenty of time to find herself a man to settle down with, to take her time getting to know him, maybe go on a few holidays. Have kids.

Twenty-nine suddenly seemed so much older. She could practically hear the clock ticking, could see her lifelong dreams beginning to fade to an impossibility. Was it time for her to change? If she was being honest with herself, her lifestyle wasn't really conducive to meeting people. She did work in a bridal shop, after all. She spent her days dealing with brides and grooms and their bridal parties. Hardly a place to meet decent, eligible men. Although, it's exactly the place Andie had met Tay.

She felt that little pang of jealousy again and pushed it aside. She shouldn't compare herself to Andie. Andie had striking auburn hair, looks that could kill, and a personality to match. Harley was ... well ... plain.

She stared at her hazel eyes, a mixture between brown, green, and a hint of gold—like they couldn't decide which single colour they wanted to be. Her face was rounded—baby-faced, as her sister, Erin, always said—with a splattering of freckles she'd never grown out of across her nose and cheeks. She'd tried different styles with her plain brown hair, but the reality of it was she couldn't stand spending hours every morning trying to beat it into submission.

She let out a sigh and got dressed, then headed to the kitchen to chase down that coffee. She stared at the light on the kettle switch as she waited for the water to boil, her fingers tapping on the bench beside her.

Was it really so bad? The thought of not finding someone, not falling in love and having that special someone love you back? Sure, it'd be like a kick to the gut considering she lived and breathed catering for happily ever afters, but her life wasn't something to be sad about. She had friends. She had hobbies. She was independent. She helped brides find that perfect gown for their perfect day, and seeing their faces when they realised they were wearing *The One*—it was priceless. Her chest tightened as the thought that she might never be that bride wearing *The One* crossed her mind. She blinked back the threatening tears and scanned her little home around her.

She had a place of her own. Sure, she was renting, but she'd been in this unit for years already and the landlord was in no rush to move her on. She had created a comfortable, warming mood with her mismatched furniture and decorations and she loved her little place. It might not be everyone's style, but it was hers. There was nothing really that she was particularly unhappy about.

Except that it all felt empty. And she felt so lonely.

And it was all since she'd met Joey.

The kettle switch clicked as it turned off, the water still bubbling inside the appliance, breaking her out of her haze. There was no use in sitting around her unit wallowing in self-pity. It was her *birthday,* for crying out loud. And

Valentine's Day or not, she deserved to spoil herself.

Deciding to have a coffee at the shops instead, she slipped her shoes on, grabbed her bag and headed to the door. She should buy something to add to her decor. Perhaps a plant to talk to might make things a little less lonely around here.

***

Joey shook out his free hand beside him and sucked in a deep breath of air, his other hand tucked behind his back. He'd been shaking in his boots by the time he'd arrived and, if Andie hadn't assured him it would be best if he waited until closer to lunchtime, he might have been here at the crack of dawn. Maybe he would have been more confident if he'd ignored her advice and shown up earlier and not allowed time for doubts to grow. He wiped his sweaty palm on his pants and had just mustered up enough courage to knock when, right before his hand could connect with the solid wood, the door swung open. And there she was.

Harley.

Her captivating eyes. Her soft brown hair, left out to rest over her shoulder. The sweet freckles. Her lush lips. His mouth went dry as he imagined kissing those lips, just as he'd imagined that—and much more—every night since he'd left.

God, he'd missed her. He hadn't realised just how much until now.

'Joey?' She'd whispered his name, but he felt his body react all the same.

He wanted to take her sweet, beautiful form in his arms and kiss her until her legs were too weak to stand. And by then, there'd be no need for standing. The scene played out in his head, and he'd almost decided it was the best way of telling her straight-up that he wanted to take things to the next level when he found himself thrusting the bunch of colourful flowers he'd carefully chosen into her arms and losing all logical thought.

'Ha-dah.' Her brows pulled together as she gingerly took the bouquet, showing him he hadn't made any sense. He cleared his throat. 'Happy day. Ha—' He snapped his mouth shut and forced himself to take a deep breath, unable to tear his gaze away from those enchanting eyes. She was even more stunning than he remembered. 'Happy birthday.'

He smiled when the words finally came out how he intended them. A smile played at her lips and he felt that twinge again. God help him. Feeling desperate for a smooth recovery, he waved a hand towards the bouquet, almost knocking it out of her arms in the process. Harley fumbled with the bouquet, managing to catch it by pressing it against her stomach. His eyes dropped to just above the colourful flowers, landing on the two creamy mounds peeking out of her low-cut top. He swallowed, bringing his gaze higher to meet hers, fighting to bring his body under control.

'They looked like you.' Her eyebrow shot up. 'I mean, they *reminded* me of you with their colours and ... stuff,' he stammered. He wished he'd written a script or something—anything to give him a better chance of wooing the pretty woman who hadn't left his dreams since he'd met her. 'They're ... well, I don't actually know what they are.' The florist had told him, but he'd be flat out remembering his own damn name at the moment.

'Gerberas,' she said quietly, her smile wide. 'They're my—my favourite, thank you.'

He couldn't resist smiling. 'You're welcome.'

'Was I ... ah ... expecting you?'

He shook his head without breaking eye contact. 'No, I—I wanted to surprise you.'

'Well, it worked.' She glanced down at the flowers in her arms. When she lifted her gaze to meet his again, there was something else in her eyes that he couldn't quite discern. His heart skipped a beat. She took a shaky breath. 'It's been a while.'

She bit into her lip and he realised what that look was. Hesitation. Worry. Awkwardness? Had he misread the signals before he'd left? Had he imagined that she might have felt the same as him in their chats afterwards? He moved a hand to reach out to her, then quickly dropped it to his side before she noticed.

'I was on the sea,' he said, matter-of-factly.

He wanted to tell her that he'd tried. That not a single day passed where he hadn't tried to contact her. That he missed hearing her voice. Missed her. But he couldn't. Not until he was certain he knew how she felt. And that she hadn't gone and got with some other guy. His eyes drifted to her supple lips, the urge to kiss them still strong. He'd almost kissed her before he'd left to go back to work all those months ago, but he hadn't. He didn't want to be the kind of guy to kiss a girl—especially one who'd just had her heart broken by some arrogant asshole—and run. He didn't want to do that to her. But he also hadn't regretted anything more in his life. The very thought that she might have found someone else in the time he was away hadn't even occurred to him until now. Joey swallowed, bringing his focus back to the present. To that flicker in her eyes that gave him some hope that maybe she felt the same way as he did.

'There's rarely reception out there,' he finished.

She held his gaze a moment longer, her mouth opening as though she wanted to say something, but nothing came out. Eventually, she sighed. 'I was just about to go to the shops. I was going to ... buy a plant, actually. Do—do you maybe want to come?'

He wasn't sure why he was surprised at her offer—wasn't that what his plan was? Deliver the flowers and spend the rest of the day with her? He smiled, his body relaxing only the slightest. At least she didn't *not* want to see him. 'Yeah, I'd like that.'

Her smile grew wide again, and he felt like anything would be worthwhile just to keep seeing that smile on her face. 'Great,' she said, nudging her thumb over her shoulder. 'I'll just pop these in some water and we can head off.' Harley started walking away, then paused, turning back to look at him again. 'It's good to see you again, Joey.'

He wanted to say something classy, some kind of smooth pickup line. But all thought left him when she looked at him like that. He smiled instead.

Chapter 3

Harley couldn't believe her eyes.

It felt like a lifetime ago since she last saw his bright brown eyes and contagious smile. And when she'd come face-to-face with the man who'd been inhabiting her mind a hell of a lot more than he probably should, she'd thought she was having some whacked-out dream. It really must have been some night for her to conjure up a life-sized Joey on the other side of her front door the next day—on Valentine's Day, no less. Her birthday.

But her head was still throbbing, and she'd already showered, so it couldn't be a dream. The only logical conclusion was that she was hallucinating. She'd seriously considered closing the door and opening it again to see if he was real, but she'd gone the path of least resistance and simply said his name—quietly enough that it wouldn't disturb her neighbours, loud enough for him to hear her. Then, taking her by surprise, he'd thrust a bouquet of beautiful gerberas into her arms.

He really was there.

And he'd remembered her birthday.

Now, as she watched him walking with the takeaway coffees towards the table she'd claimed, his dark brown hair neatly trimmed—slightly longer on top than it was on the back and sides—she still struggled to believe he'd really been there at her door. That he was here now. His eyes connected with hers as he navigated around the food court tables and he smiled. Butterflies came to life in her stomach, beating ferociously at the walls, and her heart pounded in her chest. A prickle of heat raced across her body, bringing all her nerves to attention.

It had been months since she'd heard from him—even longer since she'd seen him—and he still made her feel this way. Why would he come back now? Why wouldn't he tell her he was coming?

'Your coffee, birthday girl,' he said, sliding her coffee towards her and sitting in the chair opposite. She glanced at the tattoo on his left forearm, which she'd never noticed before—a woman dressed in a grass skirt and coconut bra.

'Thanks,' she said, wrapping her hands around the warm cardboard cup.

She took in a shaky breath. If she'd had any ideas of what to talk about before, they'd all left her now. The car ride over to the shops hadn't been eventful, filled only with short polite conversation. Most of the ride had been her stealing glances of him only to find he was looking at her, too. Then he'd smile, she'd blush, and they'd both look away. She felt like she was back in school hanging out with her crush. It was no different. She took a tiny sip of her coffee to test the temperature. Too hot to drink. She shifted in her seat, resting her elbows on the table and putting her weight forward.

'So, what are you back for?'

He stayed silent for a moment, and she might have wondered if he'd heard her if he hadn't been smiling like that, his eyes glinting with a hint of mischief. Finally, he brought his cup to his lips. 'I wanted to see you.'

She blinked, not sure if she'd heard him right. As his words replayed in her mind, she wondered if it was just one of his jokes. But then he mirrored her position, leaning forward slightly, his elbows on the table, his hands wrapped around his cup. His eyes suddenly serious.

Flustered, she said the first thing that popped into her mind. 'Seriously, though.'

His eyebrow quirked, his eyes flickering with amusement and something else that sent a delicious shiver down her spine. 'You don't think I'm being serious?'

God, she hoped he was. The thought that he might have taken leave just to see her...

But he couldn't have. No one ever did things *just for her.* She was the kind of person people caught up with if they were in town, but not the kind that people came to town for. Or, at least, that's how it had been in the past. Looking into Joey's gorgeous chocolate-brown eyes, she realised he could very well be serious. And oh, she really wished he might have come to see her, to spend her birthday—and Valentine's Day—with her as some grand romantic gesture or something of the sort. But no, he couldn't have. His sister lived in Perth. Naturally, he would have come to see Andie and thought it would be a good chance to catch up with Harley, too. After all, Andie would be a little more preoccupied now than she would have been for previous visits.

'I don't know what to think,' she said. 'We barely know each other, Joey.'

He frowned. 'We talked on the phone heaps.'

'Yeah, for the first month or so of you being away. But it's not the same as'—she pointed a finger between them—'this.'

'I tried to call as much as I could,' he said, his brow creased. 'The reception out on the sea is shoddy and—'

Joey paused, as if considering whether or not he should say what he'd been about to say. He studied her deeply, the intensity in his gaze making her heart pound harder and her breaths quicken. He ran a hand over his clean-shaven jaw, and her fingers itched to see how smooth it was. Then, seemingly coming to a decision, he took in a deep breath and reached for her hand. His warm fingers sent fire up her arm and straight to her belly, the small flame burning harder and brighter at her core. Her eyes dropped to his hand on hers, roughened from work, yet strong, broad, and deliberate.

'Not a single day passed where I didn't think about you, Harley. Where I didn't want to see you. I wanted to spend today with you. For your birthday and—and Valentine's.'

Her cheeks grew hot as he held her gaze, a flicker of hope stirring inside her. He'd thought of her. He'd wanted to see her. He hadn't forgotten about her. And, reading between the lines, maybe he felt just the same as she did.

'Is it really so hard to believe I came here for you?' he added, releasing her hand with a squeeze and returning his back to his cup.

A coolness settled over her hand, her body instantly missing his touch. When he said it like that, it wasn't so hard to believe. But now that he was no longer touching her, doubts drifted in. Had she imagined he'd touched her hand? With a heaviness, she pointed out the obvious.

'But Andie's here, too. You could have come back to see her.'

Amusement flickered across his face, but she half-suspected she saw a hint of something else, too. A sadness, or something. 'Well, she *is* my sister,' he said. 'But she has Tay now. Even staying at her place last night felt a little awkward. And I'm happy to see her, but I wanted to see you more.'

Her heart sunk a little lower. What was he saying? That he just decided to take leave to come and see her? What about when his leave was over? He'd go back to work, go back out on the sea where there's no bloody reception, and she wouldn't hear from him for months again. Then what? He'd just rock up on her doorstep again without telling her he's coming to visit?

She shouldn't feel this way about him. Shouldn't *want* him to have come for her. She couldn't even get a non-distance relationship to work out. Why should a distance relationship be any different? She swallowed, his words finally catching up to her.

'You were here last night?' She didn't know why it surprised her. Somehow, for some reason, she'd thought he must have just got in that morning.

'Yeah, I got to Andie's as she was getting ready to go out with you and Libby. You should have seen *her* reaction.'

'She didn't know you were coming either?' Andie's questioning last night suddenly made sense. She'd thought she'd been acting strange. Then again, Harley had been too drunk to really think much for most of the night.

'I didn't want her to tell you. I wanted it to be a surprise. I figured I could hang with her for the first night, then spend the rest of my leave with you. I didn't think she might have had other plans.'

A smile tugged at her lips, her heart feeling like it was going to explode at the thought that he really might have come for her. It was a strange feeling. 'And what if I had plans?' she teased.

He opened his mouth and closed it a few times, as if searching for an answer. Finally, he came up with one. 'Then I would have followed you around like a lost puppy until you agreed to hang out with me.'

'Stalker,' she jested.

'You love it.'

Yeah, she did. She bit into her lip to prevent herself from saying it. His eyes seemed to shine as he looked at her, a perfect smile gracing his handsome features. His nose was straight, his jaw square, his cheekbones defined. Though he didn't have quite the looks she had a tendency to fall for, he certainly was attractive. The way her cheeks grew hot when he looked at her like he did now only proved it. She cleared her throat so she wouldn't get stuck down the rabbit hole of processing how she felt about Joey. And how he might feel about her. She reached out a hand and touched the tattoo on his forearm, withdrawing her hand shortly after. The fire in her belly had sparked again at the contact.

'What's the significance of this?'

She had no tattoos of her own, but she'd heard that each one tended to have a meaning or some kind of significance to the person who got the ink. She hadn't seen this tattoo of Joey's last time she saw him, but now that she thought about it, he'd been wearing long sleeves or a jumper since the weather was starting to cool then. Now that it was hotter, he wore a plain dark blue tee and dark grey jeans. The outfit suited him.

'Well, it does this.' He shifted his forearm between them so she could see the grass-skirted woman better. The muscles in his forearms moved as he wiggled his fingers, making the lady shake her hips as though she was doing the hula. She had never thought of tattoos having an entertaining purpose, and yet, it was the coolest one she'd ever seen.

She flicked her gaze up to meet his. 'So you got a tattoo of a hula lady so you could make her wriggle her hips?'

'Lulu is not just any hula lady,' he said, his eyes teasing. 'She's the best hula lady this side of the equator.'

'You named her?'

'Wouldn't you?' he said, as though it made sense. She laughed, shaking her head, and he shrugged, relaxing his arm. His eyes grew serious and she realised there was more to the story. The funny larrikin Joey she'd come to know hadn't gotten that tattoo just for the amusement factor. 'My pop—Mum's dad—had one in the same spot,' he said after a few moments. 'He was more of a father to me than my own was. He's why I wanted to be a sailor in the first place. He'd been a sailor his whole career and always told me stories about his seafaring. Dad didn't like that I wanted to be like him. He wanted me to go to uni like Andie did and make something of myself.'

Harley had been about to say how stupid that was—that being a sailor *was* making something of himself. That his dad should have had more respect for him for wanting to serve his country. But she stopped herself before the words could tumble out.

'I tried it, too,' he continued, seemingly oblivious to the thoughts racing through her mind. 'I got an early entry into an economics and commerce course and studied over the summer session. And that was enough. It near on bored me to death. When Pop passed, I went out and signed up for the navy.'

She couldn't help but feel there was more to the story, but she didn't push it. 'I bet your dad wasn't happy about that,' she said before she could stop herself. His returning smile made her heart melt.

'No, he was not. That's why I stay with Andie when I'm on leave and rarely see my parents. Dad and I—we don't exactly talk much.'

'I'm sorry.'

What else could she say? Both of her parents had been on the older side when they'd had Erin, then Harley less than a year later. She'd lost her mum early—her slightly older sister basically raising her. Her dad had been a shadow of the man he used to be after that. He'd passed not long after Harley's eighteenth birthday. It was like he'd been holding on until both of his kids were raised before finally joining his beloved wife.

'It's not your fault,' Joey said, bringing her back to the present. 'Our relationship was never great to start with.'

She cleared her throat, trying to talk through the lump in her throat. 'So when did the tattoo come in?'

His smile was mischievous. 'My first pay after training. Anyway, enough about me.' He finished off his coffee and stood, holding a hand out towards her. 'Can I buy you a plant for your birthday?'

She giggled, placing her hand in his as she stood. She'd noticed the atmosphere between them change as he'd spoken. Only moments ago, it had seemed so heavy. Now, it was back to the fun, carefree aura that seemed to radiate from Joey. She let him lead her to a small shop on the outside of the shopping centre and felt the pang of disappointment when he released her hand to pick up a pot plant.

She'd missed Joey—that was for certain. And she absolutely felt things for him that she hadn't felt with anyone else. And he must feel at least *something* for her. But the thought she'd pushed to the back of her mind still niggled at her. What happens when he leaves again?

Chapter 4

Joey ducked the large plant through the front door and shifted it to one side. 'Where do you want your rubber tree?'

'It's a ficus,' Harley said, glancing over her shoulder.

His heart pounded in his chest. She'd been surprised when he showed up earlier in the day, and she'd looked like she'd had a lot on her mind. But she didn't pussyfoot around when she'd asked him over coffee why he was back in town, so he hadn't felt the need to evade the question when he answered. That's what he came here for, right? To tell her how he felt. To win her over.

Saying he'd come here for her had only been the start of that. He still hadn't gauged whether or not she'd been seeing anyone while he was away, and he wasn't entirely sure he wanted to know if she had. She hadn't believed that he would come back for her. He wondered what she'd been through—how many jerks she'd dealt with who hadn't valued her like that. Well, his girl would never feel undervalued. *His girl.* He focused on Harley's beautiful, relaxed smile. Yes, she was his girl. Even if she didn't know it yet. But she would. By the end of his leave, she would hopefully be his. And he wouldn't let her go.

'The guy who sold it to us said it's a rubber tree,' he retorted, her eyes narrowing in response. He felt a twinge again and fought the primal urge to just cart her off to her room and make love with her now. He wanted to take his time with Harley. She deserved that much.

'That's another name for the type of ficus it is,' she said, dropping her bag on the kitchen bench and walking towards a square coffee table in the corner of the lounge. 'I imagined it here.'

He placed the plant where she indicated and turned it so its best side pointed out. Then he moved back to where she was standing and admired it with her. She clasped her hands together and touched her knuckles to her chin.

'Oh, it's perfect!'

'Yeah. Perfect.'

He wasn't looking at the plant. She glanced up at him from the corner of her eye, then the rest of her head followed when she saw him looking at her. There was something about this—this moment, this feeling, her excitement—he wanted to remember it forever. Hell, he would never forget anything to do with Harley. He'd never met anyone like her, and doubted he ever would again. Call him a romantic or whatever, but he'd already fallen for the beautiful brunette. Hard.

She lifted her chin a little, her breathing shallow, judging by the rise and fall of her chest. He lifted a hand and brushed the back of his fingers across her cheek. Her lips parted, a puff of air escaping, her eyes fluttering closed. It felt as though something was pulling him towards her, and he tried his best to resist, a line of doubt settling in his mind. What if she was seeing someone he didn't know about? As far as he knew, the bastard she'd broken up with right before they'd met still lived next door. She wouldn't have gone back to him, would she?

Instinctively, he pulled back a little, his hand dropping. Her eyes shot open and he was sure he'd seen a flicker of hurt. Something tightened around his heart when he'd seen it, but as quickly as it had appeared, it was gone.

'What are you gonna name it?'

She blinked quickly, her brow furrowed. 'What?'

'The ficus.'

'I—I don't know,' she said, her voice breathy.

She took a step back, putting some distance between them, focusing back on the plant, her arms folded across her chest. He already regretted not kissing her when he had the chance. But he'd been there before with someone else. He'd been led on. He'd been hurt. He couldn't go through that again. It had been hard enough the first time. With Harley, it would break him. He couldn't risk that. He had to know before he made his move. But God, if she really was with someone else, *that* might just destroy him.

'Fleur,' she said. 'Fleur the ficus.'

With her decision made, she turned and started back towards the kitchen. Feeling his opportunity slipping through his fingers, Joey gathered up as much courage as he could to ask her before he lost his nerve.

'Do you do anyone?' Okay, maybe he should have waited a moment longer.

She stopped in her tracks and turned to face him, her eyes wide. 'Wh—what?'

'See,' he corrected, taking a breath. His heart was beating so hard and fast it felt like it was going to burst out of his chest. 'Do you—*are* you seeing anyone?'

She shifted her position, her head tilting to one side. 'No. You?'

He couldn't begin to describe the relief that washed through him. She wasn't with anyone. He regretted not kissing her even more now. He shook his head, noticing the slight smile that flickered across her face before she bit into her lower lip.

'Do you ... maybe ... want to?' God, why couldn't he get his head on straight? He'd never found words difficult. *Ever.* Yet, when he tried to tell her how he felt—or anything, for that matter—it's like he reverted to a prepubescent in that awkward-around-girls phase. He even had the tightening in his jeans to prove it.

Her eyebrow shot up, her eyes shining, and she lifted her chin. 'Joseph Gray, are you asking me out?'

'I am,' he said. 'And it's Trevor.' She gave him a confused look. 'My name. It's Trevor, not Joseph.'

'Huh,' she mused. 'Why Joey? I mean, it doesn't really come from Trevor, does it?'

'No, it doesn't,' Joey started. 'Andie has always called me Joey. Mum used to carry me around in one of those slings when I was a baby. Apparently, it reminded her of a baby kangaroo in its mother's pouch.'

Harley smiled. 'I can see how it could look like that to a child.'

'I suppose so. I never thought too much about it.' It occurred to him that he'd introduced himself to people as Joey more often than he had as Trevor lately. 'It was always her special nickname for me. I guess I've gotten used to more people calling me Joey over the years.'

'Trevor Gray.' She spoke quietly, a glaze over her eyes as though she was mulling it over. He found himself waiting for her to continue, but she simply pursed her lips, nodding slightly before returning to her journey towards the kitchen.

'So, will you?'

'Hmm?' She turned the kettle on.

'Will you have dinner with me?'

She shrugged, getting two cups out of the cupboard and putting them on the bench, her back to him. 'Sure. What do you want to order?'

He took a shaky breath, starting to close the distance between them. 'I was thinking we could go out for dinner.'

She laughed, reaching for the box of teabags. 'You know what day it is, right?'

'It's your birthday.' He reached into his pocket and retrieved the wide velvet box he'd managed to purchase while she'd been in the bookstore. A few more steps...

'No. Well, yes, but—'

'Harley.' She jumped, turning towards him. He smiled, surprised she hadn't noticed him walking towards her. His heart was pounding so hard he was sure she would have heard him. He opened the box and held it up between them. 'Be my Valentine?'

She let out a gasp as her eyes dropped to the pendant resting on the silk cushion, her hands reaching up to cover her mouth. Her eyes shimmered and her brow creased. He swallowed.

'Joey,' she whispered, moving her hands to cup the box as she stared down at the heart-shaped amethyst nestled in a ribbon of gold and tiny diamonds. 'It's beautiful.'

Her fingers brushed against his, sending a jolt of electricity through his body. His jeans grew tighter. Her mouth moved as if she tried to talk but nothing was coming out. Her gaze lifted to meet his and it took all of his restraint to not pull her into his arms and show her just how beautiful *she* was.

'Well?' he prompted.

'Y—yes, of course,' she said. 'I'd love to be your Valentine.' She glanced down at the pendant again with a longing. 'But, Joey, this is too much. I can't accept this.'

'You can, and you will,' he said simply, removing the necklace from the box. 'Turn around.'

She did as he asked, pulling her hair to one side. 'But you already bought me a plant,' she protested. He lowered the necklace around her neck and worked at the clasp.

'That was for your birthday. This is your Valentine's present.'

He finally got the clasp clipped into place and caught her scent—her shampoo, her sweet perfume, the coffee aroma. And underneath it all, *her.* He'd already lowered his head to see the clasp better. Now he was mere inches away from the delicate nape of her neck. He moved his hands over her shoulders, massaging as he went, and felt her lean back against him—just enough to bring her neck closer. He couldn't stop himself. He gently pressed his lips against the side of her neck, breathing her in, memorising her scent for those lonely nights on the sea. When he tore his lips away from her, she turned in his arms, her hazel eyes dark, her pupils dilated.

'Don't ever think you don't deserve to be spoiled,' he whispered, urging her to believe him. He lifted a hand to cup her face, his thumb gliding across her smooth cheek, and kissed her softly.

It was the most chaste kiss he'd ever experienced, and yet, it was also the most intimate. His whole body felt alive, and time truly felt like it had stopped. His heart expanded in his chest as she pressed further against him and he wrapped his arms around her, pulling her closer. The kiss only lasted a few seconds, but his body reacted so readily to the contact that they may as well have been kissing for hours. He pulled away just enough to look in her wide, bright eyes—her smile captivating, her cheeks flushed.

'Thank you,' she whispered, her voice sweet.

He smiled, pressing her harder against him. 'For the necklace, or the kiss?'

She bit into her bottom lip, still shining from their kiss. 'Both.'

'You're welcome.' Trying desperately to keep control of himself, he gave her another quick kiss and released her. 'You should change so we can go eat while we have the chance.'

She walked backwards towards her room, keeping her eyes locked with his. 'What's the alternative?' she said seductively. Oh, he could think of a few things. Determined to make her night special before going any further, he forced himself to take a deep steadying breath, his jeans growing tighter by the second.

'Patience, darling,' he said. 'You'll want to eat first.'

Her eyebrow lifted in a challenge. 'What makes you think that?'

He smiled, glad to finally know they were definitely on the same page. 'Because the food is *really* good.'

Chapter 5

Joey hadn't been lying. The food *was* good. And it might have been better if she hadn't been so distracted by the incredibly handsome, sweet, thoughtful man sitting across from her. Or perhaps that's what made the food so enjoyable. She finished off her last mouthful, placed her knife and fork on her plate, and glanced up at him, her body growing hot under his gaze. He was still wearing the clothes he'd worn earlier in the day, but he looked delicious. Surely only Joey could make jeans and a tee look *that* good.

She'd noticed the look in his eyes the second he'd turned to see her when she'd changed her clothes. Sure, she'd put on the sexiest outfit she owned—which, admittedly, wasn't totally out there. But when she'd seen his eyes darken as he followed the length of her short black strappy dress that tied around the waist and flared just below, then down her tanned legs to her chunky high heels, and back up again...

Well, she hadn't felt the way she'd felt in that moment with anyone else before. She'd been thinner the last time she'd worn this dress. She'd been worried it might not fit anymore, but the elastic in the waist was forgiving. And besides, black was slimming. She'd had to forego the bra since the deep neckline and spaghetti straps wouldn't allow for it, and she'd dug around in her underwear drawer for the lace panties she'd kept for such an occasion. They were scratchy and uncomfortable. Hell, her whole outfit had felt uncomfortable until he'd looked at her like *that.* Dark eyes, jaw tight, body tense.

For the first time in her life she felt sexy.

And suddenly the dress wasn't so uncomfortable and daring, and her panties weren't so scratchy. Though, she probably should have opted for the salad like most women would on a first date, rather than the large steak and vegetables the restaurant prided themselves on. In her defence, Joey had ordered the same. Then again, he was a man. And he could, no doubt, put away such a tasty meal with ease and not put anything on. Except maybe more muscle.

Her cheeks flushed when his lips curved in a smile. 'What?' she said, touching her napkin to the sides of her mouth in case she had food on her face. The napkin came back clean.

'It's nothing,' he said, his eyes shining.

She narrowed her eyes. 'No, tell me. Do I have something on my face?'

He shook his head slowly, leaning forward so his elbows were on the table. 'No. You look beautiful. It's just—I didn't think you'd get through all that.'

Her heart dropped to her stomach, and she tried to pretend it didn't sting a little. 'Well, I hope I didn't disgust you,' she said curtly. Had she misread the way he'd looked at her before? But surely he *liked* her. He kissed her, if her memory served her correctly. Which it did. Because it was barely a couple of hours ago. She made a move to cross her arms over her chest, feeling more self-conscious than she should, but he caught her hand before it could move far from the table.

'Harley, no. I like that you like food.'

She pouted. 'You're not making it any better,' she said quietly.

He rubbed a hand over his chin worrisomely before letting out a sigh. 'God, I can't even talk to you.'

She couldn't hold back the gasp that escaped. Was he *trying* to humiliate her? In public, no less, on the busiest restaurant day of the year. She must wear her heart on her sleeve, because he swore, his eyes wide, and he got to his feet, rounding the table until he was kneeling beside her, looking into her eyes.

'I don't mean it like that—how it sounded. What I mean is—' He paused, searching for words, his eyes not leaving hers. 'I think of what I want to say to you, and when I open my mouth, it comes out all wrong. I *like* you, Harley. More than I've ever liked anyone. And I love that you're not one of those girls who'll hardly eat anything on a date. I want you to enjoy yourself, and I can't see how not eating can be enjoyable for anyone.'

She swallowed the lump in her throat, her mind still reeling from him saying he liked her and that she made him muddle his words. She'd never thought she could have that effect on anyone. When she didn't respond, he squeezed her hand.

'Is it all coming out right, or am I still making a fool of myself?'

She shook her head slowly, her brow still creased, the back of her eyes burning from threatening tears. She searched for words of her own, but it seemed he had the same effect on her. 'So I don't disgust you?'

He chuckled, cupping her face with his hand. 'Far from it.' He kissed her then, and at the back of her mind, she thought she could hear a rumble around them. When he pulled away, his dark eyes looking deep into her soul, or so it felt, even with the big mischievous grin on his face, she realised it was not rumbling she'd heard, but clapping. 'I think they think I proposed,' he mumbled.

She laughed, her eyes growing wide. 'Really?' He nodded. Her heart fluttered at the thought of the romantic gesture. Proposing on Valentine's Day? A little cliché, sure, but romantic all the same. But he wasn't proposing, and their audience might be disappointed they'd clapped for nothing. 'What do we do now?'

His eyes narrowed in thought and he glanced towards the smaller menu left on the table. 'Don't suppose you were hoping for dessert, were you?' She shook her head, and he squeezed her hand again. 'Grab your things, then. Let's get out of here.'

He made to stand, and she pulled him back closer to her. 'Don't we have to wait for the bill?' she said.

'And what, celebrate our engagement by sitting awkwardly at the table waiting for it?'

His eyes were mischievous, and a warmth swirled in her belly at the thought of celebrating an engagement with Joey. Could they really get that serious? She shook the thought from her mind. She liked him, sure, and he said he liked her. But it was still too soon to think about love and marriage... Wasn't it?

He surprised her by giving her a quick kiss that still left her toes curling and her nerves alive, despite the shortness of it.

'No, I don't think so,' he said, pulling her to her feet. 'We'll pay at the front. Come on, beautiful.'

She slung her bag over her shoulder as he gathered up his things and led her to the front to pay, her hand in his. Her heart was still racing from his words, the way he'd called her beautiful. She planted it firmly in her mind, intending to remember it forever. Even if this—whatever this is—only lasted a short time.

***

Harley laughed as Joey led her quickly out of the restaurant and out to the street—a laugh that rippled through him and made it harder and harder to control himself. Since he'd kissed her in her kitchen, he hadn't been able to stop thinking about her luscious lips on his, her body pressing against him. How much he wanted to kiss her more, and never stop kissing her, and how he wanted to show her how truly beautiful she was.

He'd been impressed when she ordered the steak instead of conforming to what seemed to be a first-date norm among women of eating light—or barely anything. He wasn't sure what he would have done if she had done that, but he probably would have tried his best to get her to have a decent feed. But he did know he wouldn't have felt right eating that steak without knowing she could enjoy it, too. He loved that she wasn't ashamed of enjoying a meal. That she was confident enough to actually order what she wanted to eat, rather than what she thought he'd want her to eat.

And then, when he'd tried to tell her that he loved that about her, the blasted words had come out wrong. Again. And he'd seen another side of her. A vulnerable, self-conscious side of Harley Smith. And it made his heart ache. How could she not tell that she was the most incredible, beautiful woman he'd ever met? Harley should never feel self-conscious with him—not if he had any say in the matter.

They stumbled to a stop on the street, just up a little from the restaurant door, and he turned her to face him, wrapping his arms around her waist.

'All right, beautiful fiancée of mine,' he started, his heart flipping in his chest when she smiled wholeheartedly, biting into her bottom lip. 'What do you want to do now?'

Her eyebrow shot up before she brought it back to its neutral position and clasped her hands around the back of his neck. It felt so natural, so right, and yet, he still couldn't shake that self-conscious look she'd had in the restaurant from his mind.

'Hey, you asked me on the date, remember? Didn't you have it all planned out?' she teased, her eyes shining with mischief.

His lips quirked to one side. It really was no wonder he hadn't been able to get her out of his head while he was away. She wasn't just beautiful, but she made him smile like no one else had. She made him feel like he could be himself, and not have to make up stories and talk shit just to sound interesting. She brought out the Joey in him he'd been afraid to let anyone see.

The Joey who appreciated and looked after a woman in the way a gentleman should. The Joey who was a romantic and a fool for the right woman. The Joey who struggled to find the right words and things to say when she looked at him like that. The Joey who dreamed of seeing her smile again, knowing that he was the one who put that smile there. Who believed love still existed, even if he'd been hurt before.

Hell, he'd fallen for Harley more than he'd realised.

'Honestly, I didn't have anything planned,' he admitted.

Her smile softened, her fingertips teasing his hair at the back of his head. 'How come?'

She'd said it so softly he knew she wasn't annoyed that he'd taken her out without really planning anything. It was as though she sensed his hesitation. That he'd only thought to take this thing one step at a time, with the ultimate aim of winning her heart at the end of it.

'Well, I—I wasn't sure if you were going to agree to go out with me.'

She lifted her chin, pushing herself further onto her tiptoes—which wasn't much, since her heels had already given her an extra few inches. She still had to look up at him, but he didn't care. She was the perfect height for him as is.

'And why wouldn't I?' She moved closer to him, or maybe he moved closer to her. Either way, their lips were only inches apart.

'I didn't know if you'd moved on.'

She pulled back slightly, giving him a puzzled look, and he couldn't help but notice the disappointment settling in at the extra inches she'd put between them. 'What do you mean?'

'I mean, I know nothing was said when I left and we were sort of just friends, but—' He broke off, searching her eyes for any indication. Had he read too far into things when he'd left? Was this just a fling to her that only started a few hours before their date?

'But what?' she whispered, prompting him to continue.

His hands tightened around her waist. 'I've spent every day since going back to work wishing I'd said something before leaving. Knowing how I felt about you, and not knowing if you felt the same way. Not knowing if you'd find someone else.'

'I did—I *do* ,' she corrected, looking up at him with her gorgeous hazel eyes, 'feel the same way. I think.'

'Oh yeah?'

'Yeah.'

Her voice was breathless, and he noticed the faster rise and fall of her chest against his. Her fingers flexed against the back of his neck and her tongue darted out to lick her lips. He closed the distance between them, his lips firm against hers. Her arms tightened around his neck, her body pressing against him. Her lips parted against his and, if he wasn't already addicted to her before, he certainly was now. She let him in, and he searched her mouth, memorising every little bit of her he could. The feel of her in his arms, her body pressing against him.

The way her lips moved against his. Her taste. Her alluring scent. He couldn't help the groan that came when she pulled away, the look in her eyes saying what he felt inside. Her eyes fluttered as she looked up at him, a smile playing at her slightly swollen lips.

'My place or yours?'

It took a second for her words to catch up to him, but when they did, his jeans grew achingly tight. He let out a puff of air. 'Well, I'm staying with Andie so...'

'So mine it is, then.' She pulled away from him, her hand slipping into his as she led him back to her car. He couldn't help but feel that her hand belonged in his, that they were a perfect fit. When she tossed him the car keys and slid into the passenger seat, he had no hesitation in taking the shortest route possible back to her place.

Chapter 6

The heat was building in Harley's core the closer they got to her place. She'd throw glances towards Joey at the same time as he'd glance at her, flashing that lopsided smile of his that sent her insides tingling and her toes curling. It only stoked the fire even more. By the time they'd climbed the steps to her first-floor unit and she'd fumbled her keys into the lock and swung the door open, her body was only all too aware of his warm, masculine presence behind her.

She stepped into her unit, dropped her bag on the floor, and heard the door click behind them. Nerves fluttered in her belly, and her heart was racing. She swallowed. She'd been the one to initiate this. She'd wanted nothing more than to be with him as much as a woman could be with a man when he'd kissed her like that. So why was she nervous now?

She hadn't slept with anyone since, well, Angelo. And that had ended badly, especially when she'd discovered he hadn't been as exclusive as she'd thought they were. How was it possible to live next door to someone and not know he was seeing other women? Thank God he'd moved away months ago. She'd been naive and stupid then. But surely she wasn't so naive now, right?

Joey was different. He'd already said he wasn't seeing anyone else, and he'd made sure to clarify that she wasn't either. And what he'd said about wishing he'd said something before leaving...

She hadn't imagined that something was there then, and she wasn't imagining it now. But there was that small hitch of them being friends. What if they took things further and it didn't work out? Could she stand to not have him in her life at all? The last few months of not hearing from him had been miserable—and that was just based on a friendship. At some stage, he'd have to go back out on the water and she'd be left behind, waiting for the next chance they'd get to talk or see each other, not knowing when that would be.

She felt, rather than heard, him closing the distance between them. 'Do you want a drink?' she managed, hoping it didn't sound as shaky as it felt.

'Maybe later.'

He sounded a whole lot closer than she thought he was. His hands landed softly on her bare shoulders, moving down her arms slowly, his fingers teasing her sensitive inner arms. Her lips parted as a puff of air escaped and her eyes fluttered closed as she felt herself press back against his chest, his breath warm on the nape of her neck, a tingle spreading slowly through her body.

Then there was *this*. The way his fingers lit a fire everywhere he touched that travelled straight to her core, leaving her wanting more. The way he touched her so gently, so reverently, as though she was a treasure. The way he made her feel treasured, full stop. And beautiful. She knew she wasn't much to look at. She didn't have long thin legs—or a thin anything, for that matter. She was shorter than average. She had freckles and blemishes and imperfections and couldn't get her hair to truly behave no matter what she did to it.

But Joey, he … it's like he didn't see any of that. He saw her—Harley—the person inside. He knew how to make her smile and laugh and feel good about herself. And she wasn't sure she'd ever be able to find another man who could make her feel the way Joey did. Surely that meant she'd be a fool to push him away now, to deny something good from potentially blossoming because she was scared of the alternative.

He turned her slowly in his arms, his dark eyes searching hers, filled with desire. It banished any doubt that had the indecency to hang around.

'Unless, of course, you want a drink?' he said, his voice asking one question, his eyes another.

She swallowed, leaning her body harder against his, his true question pressing firmly against her belly. 'I think you know what I want.'

His chocolate eyes seemed to darken even more, and she could have sworn she saw a muscle twitch in his jaw. His hand lowered to cup her bottom and he pulled her closer again. Her hands instinctively went to his chest, his muscles hard beneath her palms, her knees already feeling weak from the chemistry passing between them.

'Tell me.'

A delicious shiver ran down her spine as his voice reverberated through her. Deep, commanding, but so, so sweet. 'I want you.'

She'd barely managed to get the words completely out before his lips were on hers, kissing her more deeply and urgently than before. All thought slipped her mind—any hint of doubt, any *what-if*s, gone. All she could think about was how this man made her feel right now, and how she'd like to feel that way every day of her life.

With a flurry of hands, both of their shoes and his shirt were ditched near the door and he lifted her effortlessly, her legs wrapped around his waist, her breasts threatening to spill from her low neckline. Their kisses grew in intensity as he carried her to her bedroom and lowered her gently on the edge of her bed.

He pulled away, slowing down, cupping her face between both of his hands. 'Have I told you how beautiful you are?'

She was speechless, her lips parting to speak, but no words forming. There was something in the way he looked at her—with such warmth and wonder—and the way he caressed her cheeks with his thumbs that brought on the realisation that maybe Joey was the thing she'd been missing the whole time.

He kissed her gently then, taking his time to explore her mouth, his hands moving from her face, caressing the natural curves of her body as they roamed over her shoulders, down her back, her sides. He circled his thumbs over her breasts, her peaks hardening beneath the thin fabric of her dress that suddenly seemed like too much to have between them. As if reading her mind, he moved lower until he reached the hem of her dress. Sliding his hands underneath, he shimmied the dress up and over her head, only breaking the kiss to move the fabric between them.

She might have been self-conscious had she not come face-to-face with a decent set of washboard abs. Her mouth went dry as her eyes followed the little trail of dark hairs leading lower. She forced herself to lift her gaze and found her hands resting on his abs, her fingers tracing every line as they moved higher. She touched her fingertips to the larger tattoo on the left side of his chest—an anchor layered over the markings of an old-fashioned compass. Every bit the man and sailor he was.

His hand lifted to cup her chin, bringing her gaze to meet his again. 'Are you sure, Harley?'

She swallowed again, trying to make her mouth not feel so dry. How could a man as handsome and kind as Joey want her? She couldn't understand it. But the way he traced his thumb over the freckles on her nose and cheeks and ran his hands through her hair...

And how he let his eyes roam over her, her body burning under his gaze, feeling more alive than she'd ever felt before...

How could she feel anything but love for the man before her?

Eventually she managed to nod, his gaze darkening further as he lowered her on the bed. 'There's only you,' she whispered.

Her eyes fluttered shut as he kissed her slowly, deeply, and moved his kisses over her neck, her collarbone, sucking her peaks into his mouth, teasing her with his tongue, and then moved lower again, doing things to her with his mouth that no man had ever done before. When her body clenched and it felt like she was literally going to explode, only then did he relent, the cool air washing over her as he moved away. And then the warmth and weight of his body was on her as he settled between her thighs, her legs wrapping around him.

'Harley, look at me.' She did as he said, his voice flowing over her as much as the tension was building inside her again. 'There's only you.'

And on those words, he entered her, filling her until she swore she couldn't have possibly taken any more, his body moving with hers as one. With each thrust and touch and kiss, she felt herself moving closer and closer to the edge until she felt herself going over, riding the waves of sweet bliss with him. And as she finally grew more aware of her surroundings and found herself curled up against Joey's side, their bodies still heaving and sweaty, her thought from before caught up to her again.

How could she feel anything but love for the man before her?

He kissed her softly, their breaths growing steady, his touch so gentle, and she knew in her heart that there was no other way to say it—no other way to describe the intensity of her feelings for this incredible man.

She was in love with Joey.

***

Something changed in the way she looked at him. No, it changed well before that. He'd seen the look in her eyes, the softness of her expression, the longing when he'd said her own words back to her.

There's only you.

Joey couldn't even begin to describe the way he felt when she'd said those words. Three simple words. Words that could mean so little, yet they'd meant so much. He wasn't sure he'd heard it the way she'd meant it, but he sure as hell knew what he meant when he said it. *There's only you.* No one else. Ever. No one else filling his dreams, his arms, his bed. No one else stealing his heart and his every waking thought. No one else he could ever love.

There might have been a time when he didn't think falling in love could happen so quickly. But the reality of it was he'd known Harley for months already. There was no one else—and he doubted there'd ever be another—he'd ever thought about as much as he'd thought of her in those months they were apart. And the moment he'd entered her and felt how right it was, how perfectly their bodies fit together like two pieces of a puzzle, he realised he didn't just like Harley all this time. He was head over heels.

She propped her chin on his chest and looked at him with those rich hazel eyes, the blue a little more prominent than before, and smiled. 'Hey,' she said.

He leaned a little closer, meeting her lips with his. He'd never get enough of kissing her. Never get enough of feeling her in his arms, her naked body against his. 'Hey, beautiful.'

Her cheeks flushed a deeper pink and he felt that tug in his chest. How could she still not think she was beautiful? How could she not see what he saw? Her fingertips traced along the tattoo on his chest. He'd seen how she'd looked at it before, yet she hadn't said anything about it. She still didn't now. Instead, she patted her hand against his chest and propped herself on her elbow.

'So that was ... um ... something.'

He held back a scoff. *Something* was an understatement. 'Disappointed?'

Her eyes went wide. 'No, of course not. I just—I wasn't expecting ... this.'

'And what might that be?' He knew what she meant. Or at least, he thought he did. Truth be told, he hadn't quite expected this either—how intense it was, to be more specific.

'This. Us. You.' She worried her lower lip with her teeth, and he resisted the urge to kiss her again for fear of distracting her. She let out a long breath. 'I woke up this morning feeling miserable and hungover and now...' Her fingers started tracing the tattoo again as she gathered her thoughts. He waited. 'I wasn't sure I'd see you again. And today, of all days.' Her brow creased, a slight smile playing at the corners of her lips. 'You remembered my birthday.'

He cupped her cheek in his hand, brushing his thumb over those sweet freckles. 'How could I forget?'

'I thought you had. Forgotten me, that is.'

He couldn't resist kissing her again—soft, slow, deliberate. When he broke away, he rested his forehead against hers. 'You're too good to forget.' Her smile was genuine, but she was still holding something back. He frowned, pulling himself up so he was resting against the bedhead. 'What's on your mind?'

'How long do we have?' she said, her voice so quiet he had to make sure he'd heard her correctly.

'Until I go back?' She nodded, and he let out a long breath. He'd tried not to think about it, but he knew it would come around. No matter what, time would always still happen. 'I leave next Sunday.'

'A week,' she breathed, her face dropping. Her eyes shimmered with unshed tears and her cute little nose crinkled. His chest ached with her. 'That's all I get? I don't hear from you for months and I only get a week with you?'

'That's the life, Harley,' he said, wishing it really wasn't. 'I can only really take leave in intervals. The ship was docking, so the timing was right. We go back out in a week. I—I would have taken longer if I could.'

She sniffed, dropping her gaze. 'Will you have reception?'

He shook his head slowly, wishing he could make this easier. The lifestyle involved with his career had never been an issue before. Then again, he'd never had a reason to want to spend more time on land. Until now.

But he couldn't just change that. The navy had been his life for all of his adulthood. He was born to be a sailor—he'd always known that. It's what he was good at. It's what he knew how to do.

'I don't know,' he said honestly. 'Sometimes we have reception and oftentimes, nothing. It depends on where we go.'

She glanced up at him, a lone tear rolling down her cheek. He wiped it away with his thumb and lowered his hand to hold both of hers in both of his.

'Is it dangerous?' she whispered, seemingly holding her breath.

'There's always a risk.' He wasn't going to start lying to her now. His job wasn't easy. For the most part, he hadn't been in danger. But that didn't mean it would always be the case.

'So we get a week, and then what?'

He brought her hands to his lips and held them there a moment, only pulling them away to talk. 'And then we figure out the next step.'

She smiled, but she didn't seem entirely convinced. 'You're not much of a planner, are you, Joey?'

He shook his head and pressed his lips to hers. He poured everything he had into it and hoped she could tell. There were some things that just couldn't be said with words. He cupped her face between both hands and urged her to look at him.

'I know this,' he said. 'What we have. It's special. And I don't want to lose you. But I understand it's not the life for everyone. Just ... don't break my heart, okay?'

She let out a sob, her hand reaching up to cover her mouth as she shook her head, squeezing her eyes closed. 'I don't want to, Joey.'

'Hey,' he said, urging her to open her eyes again.

When she did, all he saw was raw emotion. No matter what, he couldn't let her slip away. She was a practical woman. And he knew he'd be pushing it to ask her to wait for him. But he sure as hell wasn't going to spend the rest of the week in misery, the end of their time together nearing and taunting them. He wanted to enjoy this week with her. Even if she decided she couldn't do long-distance with him, that the circumstances would be too hard. It would break him if that happened. But he wanted to spend every waking moment with her before he left.

'Come away with me.'

'What?'

She looked surprised. It surprised him, too. He had no plan of where they'd go or what they'd do. But hell, if taking her away somewhere was the only way he'd get to spend as much time with her as he could and make it truly memorable, then so be it.

'Come away with me.'

Chapter 7

Harley wasn't sure she'd heard him right. Then he'd said it again. *Come away with me.* She could have sworn her heart stopped beating. The thought that they only had a week together—in which time she still had to work—well, she'd known his visit was limited. But a *week?* A week of what, making love and getting attached and then he'd be gone for God knows how long? She couldn't do that!

She was already too attached to him as it was. She would already be miserable when he left again, and they'd only spent the day together. She had never felt like this with any other man. She'd never felt cherished and spontaneous and *loved* by any other man. Joey had completely and utterly ruined her for anyone else. And the only thing she regretted was that he'd have to leave again. She knew that she wouldn't see him for months—likely not even hear from him for much of that time. She would never be able to move on from this man. But she also wasn't sure she could deal with not hearing from him or seeing him for so long.

'Name a place, and we'll go.' He was sitting upright now, his expression excited. She struggled to sort out her thoughts.

'What? Joey, are you crazy?'

His eyes glinted with mischief. 'Maybe I am. So be crazy with me. Harley, we have a *week* together.'

He said it as though it sounded like a long time. But she knew that if she went away anywhere with him, she'd only be more of a lost cause. But if she didn't...

'Where's somewhere you want to go? We can spend the week there, enjoy each other, and not think about us being apart after it.'

'But we can't.' She forced the words out, but she wasn't entirely convinced. They couldn't, could they?

'Why not?'

She stammered. 'I have to work, for starters.'

'Call in sick.'

'I'd need a medical certificate for that long.'

'Call in a favour?'

She shook her head. 'Joey, I—I can't. This is all happening too quickly. Can't we just enjoy this? Now? How we are?'

He tried to hide the disappointment from showing on his face, but not before she'd caught it. It was the right thing to say, wasn't it? They *couldn't* just go away. People didn't just do that. *She* couldn't just do that. He might be on leave for the week, but she still had appointments with clients coming out her ears. Finally, he smiled, pulling her into his arms.

'Yeah, of course, darling. Anything you want.'

She pouted into his chest. It wasn't about what she wanted. She never got what she wanted. She wished that, for once, she *could* get what she wanted. And for now, that was to keep Joey here, in her bed, making sweet, sweet love and to keep feeling his touches, his kisses. Feeling that slow burn through her body and pretending that he wasn't going anywhere.

***

Her wishes came true—for the night, at least—and then she had to snap back to the harsh reality of working life. She'd dropped Joey back at Andie's the next morning where his spare clothes were and managed to get to work only ten minutes late. As soon as she walked through the door of *Bride and Beau*—a clever name for a bridal shop, she'd thought—and blinked through the blissful haze hanging around her, she knew something was wrong. A few tradesmen walked past her with a huge pane of glass while others cleaned the shattered glass on the floor. Men and women in police uniforms seemed to be examining every inch of the shop. Her boss, Jannette, was talking to a man in a brown suit who had a notepad. She looked stressed, probably for a good reason. Harley scanned the room until she found Andie frantically manning the phone, making and answering calls. She beelined towards her.

'Hey, what's going on?'

Andie's eyes were wide as she hung up the phone. 'Haven't you heard? It's all over the news.'

She shook her head, feeling a pang of guilt that she hadn't heard anything. Joey had been keeping her so busy and distracted that she hadn't even thought that anything else might have happened.

Andie's eyes followed a young policeman searching through the racks of expensive gowns. Harley flinched. Jannette would not like the way her things are being handled. Andie reached for Harley's arm and pulled her close.

'We were broken into last night. They don't know who it was.'

Harley couldn't believe her ears. 'Did they take anything?'

'Some of the expensive jewellery. But that's not what they're worried about.' Harley gave her a look to go on, not able to form any words. Andie leaned closer again. 'They're looking for something that doesn't belong. Something they might have left behind. I've only heard rumours—something about possibly being related to that string of break-ins.'

'You think it could be?'

Who would break into *Bride and Beau?* They were one of the more modest shops in the street, one that really didn't draw that much attention. She racked her brain. Had she seen anyone looking suspicious recently? Harley searched her mind for anyone who might not be happy with her boss or the business. She couldn't think of any unhappy customers, and she couldn't think of anyone in Jannette's personal life. True, she didn't know much about her personal life. Still, the break-in alone would damage the business. Surely this was connected to the other break-ins in the area she'd heard about. A mystery robber who seemed to always leave some kind of contraband behind. She'd thought it was all just hearsay.

'I don't know,' Andie whispered, standing straight as Jannette and the man in the brown suit neared them.

Harley still couldn't believe all that was going on. No doubt she'd have to put in more time that week to get everything in order. She tried to push aside the sadness that the extra hours at work would be cutting into the little bit of time she still had with Joey.

'Oh, Harley, you're here,' Jannette said, looking slightly relieved, but also weary. 'You don't know who could have done this, do you?'

Harley noticed the man eyeing her suspiciously. 'No, of course not,' she said, hoping she didn't sound defensive.

She *didn't* know. And she *shouldn't* sound defensive. But there was just something about police and detectives that made her nervous and feel like *she* was the suspect. Judging by the way Andie held herself, she probably felt the same.

'Everything's going to be okay though, right?' she added, avoiding the man's gaze—she was sure his eyes had narrowed as he studied her.

'We don't know,' Jannette said, looking to the man. 'Detective Attler?'

'We have cause to believe this may have been a targeted attack,' Detective Attler said, finally sharing his gaze between the three of them. 'There's no telling if it'll happen again, or worse.'

'Which is why,' Jannette tagged on, 'we need to close down for a while.'

Harley swallowed, glancing at Andie. She didn't look surprised. Maybe

Jannette already mentioned it as a possibility to her, since she would have been at work on time. The detective excused himself to go talk to a senior policeman.

'Close down? For how long?' Harley said.

'Until the culprits have been caught, I suppose,' Jannette said. 'And we've made sure there's no danger. I think it would do us all good to have a few weeks off regardless. You'll still be paid, of course. Consider it bonus leave. Andie, you've cancelled all client appointments for the next few weeks?'

'I have,' Andie said. 'The brides are all very sorry to hear about what happened.'

Jannette nodded solemnly. 'Well.' She let out a sigh, looking around them. 'I'll get some professionals in to clean up after the police have finished their thing. You two don't need to hang around. Go enjoy the rest of your day.'

Harley still couldn't believe what had happened overnight. Trust something bad to happen the night that something good actually happened to her. The break-in was devastating, and not knowing what will happen with the store that was already struggling to keep afloat—what would happen with her job—made it all worse.

But another part of her—a smaller, more selfish part of her—focused on the fact that she now didn't have to worry about going to work for the next week. She felt horrible for even thinking it, but she couldn't help but feel a bit happier that she could spend more time with Joey in his week off.

She just wished it hadn't come at such an expense.

***

'Margaret River?'

'Well, hello, beautiful.'

Joey pulled the beautiful brunette into his arms and kissed her. It had only been a few hours since he'd seen Harley, but God, it seemed to drag on for days. It didn't make much sense—he'd spent months on end away from her and, while it was still hard to be away for so long, it didn't seem to take as long as those past few hours did. But still, she'd gone to work. And he was pretty sure her workday was a lot longer than a few hours. He glanced up and down the street and pulled her into the house with him.

'You better come inside before my fiancée sees you. She could be here any minute.'

Harley laughed—a sound he could never tire of. 'Oh, stop it!'

She slapped him playfully on the chest and pushed herself up on her tiptoes to kiss him. He registered the fact she was wearing very different clothes—and a lot less formal—than she was when she'd dropped him back at Andie's place that morning.

'So, what do you think?' she said, her eyes wide. 'Still keen for that week away?'

He tilted his head to the side, pulling back just enough to study her face. 'I thought you had to work.'

'Well, I did, but there was this break-in last night and now Jannette's given us a few weeks off to give the cops a chance to find out who's responsible—'

'Wait,' Joey said, shaking his head. God, she could talk fast sometimes. 'A *break-in* ?'

'Yeah, I mean, it sucks, and we don't know what's going to come of it, but for now, I have the next few weeks off.'

He could tell the news of the break-in saddened her, but at the same time, she seemed relieved—elated, even. Hell, he couldn't stop himself from feeling happy that she no longer had to work for the next week. The fact it was because of a robbery only made him feel guilty about feeling happy.

But love was a complicated thing, wasn't it?

Harley's expression grew serious. 'You didn't mean it,' she whispered.

'Of course I meant it,' he said, pulling her close again. 'I mean everything with you. But are you sure? You won't be needed back at the bridal shop?'

'Jannette seemed pretty serious about us taking time off. She looks like she could do with it herself. And if she needs anything, I'm sure Andie can take care of it while we're gone.'

'You're probably right about that,' he mused. His sister was one to be there whenever she was needed.

'So...?' Harley prompted, wiggling her eyebrows.

'So let's do it,' Joey said, planting a kiss on her lips. 'You and me. Margaret River. Are you packed?'

She nodded, biting into her lip, her eyes shimmering with excitement. 'I wanted to leave as soon as we could.' He was certain he hadn't imagined her cheeks turn a shade pinker.

He pulled away, giving her arms a squeeze as he did, excitement building inside him. He'd never gone anywhere with a woman before—not like this. Not a spontaneous trip for a week to be alone with her. No interruptions. No work. Just Harley. To be honest, the trip felt long overdue. He just hoped she felt the same.

'I'll grab my things.'

Chapter 8

Joey listened to the sounds of the ocean as the early morning light filtered in through the slit between the curtains. It was almost dark when they'd arrived at the beachside cabin in Margaret River, but Joey wouldn't have traded it for anything. Seeing Harley's excitement in every town they went through, that they just *had* to see more of, filled Joey's heart even more. And the more it filled, the more he fought the thought at the back of his mind that he'd be leaving again soon. And how leaving might just hurt more than he was willing to admit.

He focused on the roar of the sea outside and Harley's steady, even breathing as he held her naked body against his. Two of his favourite things. He couldn't help but feel that he was exactly where he belonged and yet, at the same time, he felt torn. How could he belong here when his place was on a navy ship somewhere out on the water? The same water he could hear now. The navy lifestyle wasn't conducive to family life. But he didn't have that, did he? This thing with Harley ... it was real. But it was also new. And he knew she was already worried about what would happen when he had to leave. But they still had the rest of the week to enjoy before they had to figure it out. And the week had only just begun.

He felt Harley stir in his arms and he pressed a kiss to her forehead. 'Mmm,' she hummed, stretching her body against his. 'What are you thinking about?'

'How peaceful it is here,' he said, tracing patterns on her back with his fingertips. 'You hear that?'

'The waves?'

'Yeah.'

She propped herself up a little, resting her chin on his chest. 'I suppose you'd hear that all the time, wouldn't you?'

He shook his head slowly, his thoughts drifting back to his ship. 'It's different. You can hear everything here. The waves crashing on the shore. The birds. The calm. The only place you can really hear the water out there is if you're on the deck and, even then, the sound is dampened by the roar of the ship. It's not like this.'

Harley let out a long, slow breath. 'I never thought of it like that. I thought it would still sound the same.'

'I did too,' Joey admitted, twirling a lock of her hair around his finger. 'It wasn't until I went out on the ship the first time that I realised I hadn't even thought about ship noises.'

'What's it like out there?' Harley moved her fingers over his chest, tracing the patterns on his tattoo. 'You must like it.'

'Yeah, I do.' He watched her fingers move, following each line of his tattoo. 'It took a bit of getting used to—going from being on land all the time to suddenly living on the water. But I love it. And you're with the same people all the time. They become your family. I couldn't imagine doing anything else.'

Her fingers stopped moving and she shifted so she was no longer looking at him, but he hadn't missed the disappointment that flickered over her face. She took a breath and held it in as though she was readying herself to say something, then let it out slowly.

Joey released the lock of hair and ran his hand over her back, memorising the feel of her in his arms. He knew the line that must be running through her head. He'd heard it from some of the guys on the ship who'd had women say it to them. Did he have to go back? Couldn't he do something different?

Navy life didn't make relationships easy, and maybe he'd been a fool to think that it could be different for him. But there was something about Harley that gave him hope that maybe they could work it out. Surely Harley wouldn't expect him to give up his job—his life. She wasn't that kind of woman, was she? Before he could break the silence, his stomach rumbled, and Harley laughed, pulling herself upright.

'We should find some food,' she said, wrapping the sheet around her as she slid off the bed. 'What do you think?'

'I think nothing would be open yet.'

'You're probably right. Shower then food?' She gave him a mischievous look that had his heart pounding in his chest and his body rising to attention. 'A very *long* shower?' She backed herself towards the bathroom then, as she turned her back towards him, let the sheet fall to the ground.

A different kind of hunger filled him and, with a rumble starting at the base of his throat, he rolled off the bed and followed her. They could deal with the end of the week when they got there. For now, he intended on enjoying every moment he had with Harley. Starting with that shower.

***

'I once got stuck up a tree because I was trying to save some baby birds I thought were in trouble.'

'Wait, how old were you?'

Harley tangled her fingers with Joey's as she rested against him, his arm around her as they stared out at the rolling waves. His words from early that morning still niggled at her—*I can't imagine doing anything else*—and the questions still filled her mind, despite trying to push it all aside. What would happen when he goes back to work? What would become of them? Could she manage a relationship like this—of marvellous weeks spent together and long months apart? It would be hard, but there was something different about Joey. She wasn't sure she could deal with being separated from him if they stayed together, and yet the thought of letting him go was agonising. But she couldn't let herself dwell on it. Couldn't let it ruin the little time they had together.

'I was four,' Joey said, reaching for a chip from their takeaway lunch.

She'd never thought fish and chips could taste so good, but as she and Joey were eating on the beach, she wasn't sure she'd ever had a better meal in her life. There was something about hiding their food from the lurking seagulls, watching the waves move in and out, enjoying the sea breeze and overall simplicity of lunch with the man she'd fallen for.

'And were they? In trouble?' She watched a surfer ride the waves in the distance. The beach wasn't exactly secluded, but they'd managed to find a quiet shady spot off to the side of the popular part where they were relatively left alone.

'Nah, just hungry. When Dad finally got me down, the mother bird swooped in and fed them.'

'How long were you stuck for?'

'Felt like hours, but was probably only a few minutes, tops.' Joey laughed, pressing his cheek against the top of her head.

It felt so right to be in his arms. But at the same time, she couldn't help but think it was all going so fast. He'd only come back a couple days ago, for starters, and he'd been in her bed that first night.

Was it fast though?

She *had* known him for close to a year, and she'd been friends with his sister for a lot longer. What about Andie and Tay? They were in love and settled into their relationship within a few months. And what about everyone else? What about the people who start a relationship on a one-night stand? Surely *this* wasn't fast.

But she'd already fallen for Joey, and there was nothing to say that this wasn't all just a bit of fun on his time off. Sure, he'd said that he came back for her, and she wanted to believe that.

But for only a week? How was she supposed to fully enjoy the week, to let herself feel for this guy, and still keep herself distant enough that the pain wouldn't be unbearable when he left?

'Well, I think it's cute that four-year-old you was so concerned about the baby birds,' she managed, pushing the thoughts aside.

'I was always getting into trouble one way or another. Always doing things Dad didn't approve of.'

She glanced up at him. He was staring out at the water, his eyes distant. 'Do you still talk to your dad?'

'Only if I see him, which isn't very often.'

She sat up straight to face him, still holding his hand in hers. He'd brushed over the topic last time it was brought up, but so much had happened since then. And they didn't have much time to truly get to know each other, so she wanted to make the most of it.

'What happened?' she asked.

Joey tore his eyes away from the water to look at her. The look in his eyes made her breath catch in her throat. Sorrow. Pain. Hurt. Anger. He dropped his gaze, reaching for another chip that she was sure had gone cold long ago.

'Ah,' he started. 'It's a long story.'

'I've got time.'

'Mmm. How about the shortened version?' She nodded. At this point, she would take anything to get to know the man she felt so strongly for. 'He's convinced I'm not his child.'

He turned his gaze towards Harley, a darkness in his eyes. The pain she'd seen there made sense. 'D—did you get tested?'

He stared down at his foot pressing into the picnic blanket in front of him. 'Nah. Mum said there was nothing to prove, that I was his son, and if he didn't believe her, he didn't trust her. Why should she have to prove that she'd never had an affair?' His jaw tightened and she squeezed his hand, her thoughts drifting to how Joey would have felt growing up, knowing his father didn't think of him as his own child. As if reading her mind, he continued. 'It's like he never even wanted me. I obviously took after Mum's side of the family more than I did his, but still.

He's my dad. He was supposed to be my hero, my role model and all that shit. He never even threw a ball with me. Just acted like my existence was a thorn in his side.'

Harley swallowed, deciding on her next words carefully. 'It must have been hard.'

'It was. I mean, I'd never treat my kids—mine or not—like that. No kid deserves to feel like an outsider to his own family.'

He lifted her hand and pressed his lips against the back of her fingers, still not looking at her. She couldn't help but wonder if he'd linked thoughts of his kids with her. Did he feel as deeply for her as she did for him, then? She took in a deep breath as he returned both of their hands to her lap.

'I get why your mum didn't want a DNA test,' she started. 'I also get how that could make it look like she had something to hide. But he shouldn't have treated you like that.'

He turned towards her, his eyes saddened. 'What if it was you, Harley? What if your husband didn't believe your kid was his?'

She swallowed the lump in her throat, trying to ignore how the way he'd said *your husband* made her feel like he didn't think it would be him. She held his gaze, not daring to break the contact. 'I'd get the DNA test. I'd have nothing to hide, and if it was best for the kid if we got the test, I'd do it. I couldn't bear the thought of my kids not having both of their parents.'

'Did you?' he asked, his eyes softening. 'Have both of your parents?'

She shook her head, the ache building inside her whenever she thought of her parents. 'I was young when Mum died. Too young to have many memories. But I remember that Dad became a different man. It's like he was there, but wasn't. He wasn't very involved, only there for the basics. Distant. My nanna helped out for the first few years, but then she was gone, too. Erin—my sister—practically raised me after that, even though she wasn't much older than me.'

'Is your dad still around?' He asked the question, but Harley half-suspected he already knew the answer.

'Dad died when I was a little over eighteen. And of course I miss him, and I miss Mum, but we weren't very close. I sometimes wonder if he thought that if he never got close to us, that we wouldn't hurt so much when he wasn't around anymore.'

'But you would have preferred to be close.' It wasn't really a question.

Harley nodded and Joey pulled her back into his arms again, kissing the top of her head. The butterflies stirred in her stomach like they did every time she felt his kisses. 'I'd rather love and lose than never love at all.'

As she said it, she realised the truth in it. And how it didn't just apply to her parents.

Chapter 9

'I can't believe you got us horses!'

Joey glanced at the huge animal walking beside him who stared back and snorted. He was starting to regret his rash decision, but Harley had seemed so excited when he'd found that brochure about beachside horseriding. It had sounded romantic at the time. Now, the thought of pulling himself up onto the back of this huge, black, snorting beast and riding it didn't sound so appealing. The horse he was supposed to ride was called Bucky—not at all a reassuring name—and Harley's slightly smaller brown horse was Bay.

'Anything for my fiancée,' he teased, catching a glimmer of amusement in her eyes. 'I'm glad you're enjoying yourself.' He hazarded a pat on Bucky's neck. The horse went for a nudge at Joey's arm and he stepped just out of reach.

'You okay?' Harley said. He moved his head only slightly to see her better, still certain he couldn't take his eyes of the conniving creature.

'Ah, yeah. I'm good. You?' He hoped that she hadn't noticed his hesitation and rejoiced a little inside when it looked as though that was the case. She let out an excited squeak and Bucky paced beside him.

'I haven't ridden in so long. Nanna used to take me and Erin horseriding when we were little. I've only had the chance to ride maybe once or twice since.'

She turned to look at him fully, her horse completely out of her field of vision, he noticed. His heart pounded in his chest. This was a stupid idea. What on earth possessed him to think that trying to control two huge horses would be safe and fun? If Harley got hurt...

'Have you ridden before?' she said, her eyes flashing with excitement.

'Me? Yeah. Of course. Heaps of times.' *Try never.* Truth was, apart from those little ponies in the occasional petting zoo at markets, Joey had never even been near a horse before. Bucky deviated off course and pressed against him, making Joey's heart pound even harder. This was a very, very bad idea.

'Shall we hop on, then?'

'We should probably keep warming them up,' Joey said, putting some distance between him and Bucky again.

'I think they're warm enough,' Harley said, her eyebrow lifting as she pulled to a stop. Bay moved in front of her so Harley was closer to the saddle. 'Come on, don't you want to feel the wind in your hair?'

'Sure.' He ran a hand through his short hair. He doubted he could feel the wind in his hair like she probably would. But if he could, riding a horse to feel it wasn't a particularly appealing option.

But what choice did he have? He stopped walking and, unlike Bay, Bucky stopped where he was. By the time he'd moved closer to the saddle and glanced back at Harley to see how to mount a horse, she was already settling herself in the saddle. He sighed, put both his hands on top of the saddle, and jumped, attempting to pull himself up. Bucky moved sideways, and Joey landed back on the ground. God, he wished he'd seen how Harley got up. He tried it again and, once more, he got nowhere. Bucky pushed against his arm with his head and Harley laughed.

'Don't tell me you've never used a saddle before,' she teased.

'You could say that,' he mumbled, risking a glance at her.

Harley's eyebrow shot up. 'Mmm, there's something sexy about a man riding bareback.'

'Yeah, well my bareback methods aren't working with Bucky, so care to explain?'

'Use the stirrup,' Harley said. He looked at her blankly. 'The foot thing.' She moved her foot to emphasise her point.

'Right.' He put his foot in the stirrup and she laughed again.

'You'll get nowhere or end up backwards if you do that. Try your other foot and turn the stirrup around. It's twisted.'

He did what she said and hopped alongside the horse as Bucky took a few staggering steps. 'Now what?'

'Now get up. Grab onto the pommel and swing your other leg over.' When he stared at her, she tapped on the hump at the front of her saddle. 'This thing.'

Taking a big breath, he swung his leg up and wobbled into the seat, gripping the pommel. Bucky took a few steps and Joey slid over, landing flat on his back on the other side of the horse. Bucky spun his head around to look at Joey and snorted in his face. Great. Just how he'd imagined their romantic beachside horseriding date would go. Harley walked her horse towards him and stopped where she could see him.

'You okay?'

'Yup,' he said, already feeling his bruised ego. He pulled himself to standing and stared at Bucky, who nudged against him again.

'Might want to have the reins up there next time,' Harley mused.

'Right. That would make sense.'

He made no move for the horse, wondering what the hell the reins were. Harley leaned to the side towards Bucky and Joey's heart leapt into his throat at the thought that she might be slipping off. But then she rose again, the leather straps attached to Bucky's harness in her hands. She swung them over Bucky's head and sat them over the pommel.

'Try that,' she said.

He marvelled at the skill she had to be able to adjust his horse while still on her own, but he said nothing so she wouldn't know it was his first time riding a horse. He tried again, and to his relief, he landed securely in the saddle. It wasn't as comfortable as he'd imagined it might have been, but he was there.

'Let's go,' Harley said, riding Bay with effortless ease. He had to admit, she did look good on a horse. He watched her and Bay move as though synchronised and knew he and Bucky wouldn't look anywhere near as good.

He gave the reins a little flick and Bucky did nothing. 'Come on, man. You're making me look bad.' Bucky gave another snort and nodded his head. 'You're doing this on purpose, aren't you?'

Another snort. Great. Too bad if he was trying to impress Harley. He supposed there were actually things that he couldn't just wing and hope he did well enough to get by. Horseriding was one of those things. He tried a series of hushed voice commands, tapped the side of the horse's neck, and all he got in return were snorts and the occasional stagger.

'Having issues?' Harley called back, turning her horse to see him.

'Just finding the gears,' he joked. 'We'll catch up.'

Her laugh mingled with the sounds of the waves coming in, carrying across the air between them and rippling through his body. No, he could never tire of her. 'Try the foot pedals,' she said.

'Foot pedals? What'—he held his feet tucked in the stirrups out to the side—'these things?'

Harley gave him a thumbs up and he sighed. He really was making a fool of himself, wasn't he? He let his feet drop back to the horse's side and Bucky lurched forward at a run. In a few seconds, they'd overtaken Harley and her horse, and it looked as though Bucky had no intention of slowing down. Deciding he had to just let the horse run it out, Joey concentrated on holding on for dear life and not falling off the beast running a million miles an hour. He wasn't sure how he managed to stay on or how the hell Harley had caught up to him, but she was soon there, laughing and telling him to pull on the reins. Trying his best to keep balance without hugging Bucky's neck, he pulled back on the reins and the great beast slowed to a walk. After a few moments, Joey's heart slowly returned back to its normal pace and he no longer felt like he was going to fall off with every jerk. Well, talk about an experience. He glanced over at Harley and couldn't resist the warmth spreading through him.

Her hair was messy, her cheeks pink from the wind, her eyes wild with excitement, and her smile irresistible. It really was no wonder he'd fallen for this beautiful woman, and he still couldn't believe that she wanted to hang out with him.

'So how are you finding your first ride?' she said, her eyes teasing.

'It's not—' Her eyebrow shot up and he sighed in defeat, laughing. 'Is it that obvious?'

'Just a little,' she said, biting into her lip.

As their horses walked side by side, Joey found it easier to let Bucky take control and trust that he wasn't going to rear up and dump him in the sand. He studied Harley's frame and how natural she looked sitting on her horse. It really was something she loved—he could see it in her eyes. But he also wondered why she didn't do it more often. Perhaps it was harder to find horses to ride in Perth than it was in Margaret River. Or perhaps the thought hadn't even crossed her mind. He wondered if it was one of those things she'd forgotten she loved until she did it again.

'And you had me thinking you were so experienced you rode bareback,' Harley teased, bringing his thoughts back to the present.

'You're the one who said it was sexy,' he said. 'How could I say no to that?'

She reached across and gave his shoulder a shove. 'You're a dork.'

He caught her hand before she could retrieve it and laced his fingers with hers. 'And you love it.'

She bit into her lip, her cheeks reddening. 'Yeah, I do.'

He held her gaze and admired the way the setting sun sent a golden glow over her face, catching in the copper streaks of her brown hair, making the hint of gold in her eyes stand out. She really was the most magnificent thing he'd ever seen.

'Have I told you today that you're beautiful?' he whispered, releasing her hand to reach across and tuck a lock of hair behind her ear.

'You did this morning,' she said, her cheeks darkening even further.

His thoughts flickered back to the way he'd made love to her that morning and his body twitched in response. They were heading into their third night at Margaret River and he felt like he'd give anything to turn those final few nights into a lot more. He somehow managed to angle Bucky closer to Bay and leaned in to Harley.

'Then I haven't said it enough.'

She leaned towards him and he closed the distance between them, covering her mouth with his. He kissed her passionately, pouring everything he wanted to say into it and hoping she got the message. She parted her lips, letting him in, and he felt that now-familiar rumble at the base of his throat. She tasted sweet, addictive, and there was no way in hell he could ever get enough of her.

A little too late, he realised the distance was growing between the rest of his body and hers and he released her only to land in the sand between them. Her laughter seemed to vibrate in the air around him and he smiled. If that was how he was going to go, it wouldn't be so bad.

Chapter 10

'Okay, if you could do anything, what would it be?'

Harley reflected on the previous few days as she sipped her glass of wine on the veranda of their cabin. Their exploration of the town of Margaret River earlier that day. Their beachside horseriding the evening before. The romantic strolls and heart-to-hearts they'd had in their time away. With every passing moment, she felt herself growing closer to Joey, felt whatever it was between them grow stronger and stronger.

It had long since gone dark, but she could still see the light from the moon and stars reflecting on the water. She still couldn't believe Joey had managed to find them a beachside cabin. To see that view and hear those sounds every moment of every day—well, that would be a dream come true. And it was. The very idea of spending a week in a place like this with a man like Joey was only ever something she'd dreamed about. And yet, here they were, sipping wine on a porch swing together, listening to the rumble of the tide, breathing in the crisp sea breeze. So when Joey asked what she would do if she could do anything, the very thing they were doing came to mind.

'I'd do this,' she said, snuggling into him as he traced patterns on her arm. 'Stay here. With you.'

She glanced up at him to find him focused on her. It was too dark to see his eyes clearly, but she felt it. Felt the way the intensity in his gaze bored through her, reaching her deepest, most sensitive inner parts.

'That would be nice,' he whispered, sending a delicious shiver down her spine. 'But I meant as a job. If you could do anything, would you still be a seamstress in a bridal shop?'

Harley stared back out at the water, taking a deep breath. That day had been the first time in their whole trip where she hadn't thought that very question. The break-in at the shop was still a scary thought. What if Jannette decided to close for good? They were already struggling to keep afloat as it was. Throw the break-in on top of that and, well, it really wasn't looking good. Harley knew that Jannette wouldn't fire either her or Andie if she could avoid it. They made a great team, and Jannette needed the two of them to keep things running smoothly. So it was all or nothing. At the end of the time off, she would either still have a job, or she may very well be without one.

And what would she do then? She had some money saved up, so she would be okay for a while. And she was sure Erin would help her if she desperately needed it. Still, she'd hate to be in that kind of position.

'I've always been a seamstress,' she muttered. 'Andie could probably tell you that. We've worked together for so many years. I don't—I don't know what I would do if I couldn't do that. It's what I'm good at. What about you?'

He took a moment to respond, but she already knew what his answer would be. Being a sailor was as much a part of him as being a seamstress was to her. 'I always dreamed of being a sailor,' he said, squeezing her gently. 'If I couldn't do that ... I don't know. I suppose I would try to use my degree somewhere. I wouldn't even know where to start.'

'What's your degree?' Harley said, realising that she never knew he *had* a degree, let alone what he did on his ship.

'Electronic engineering. I got it as part of my training when I signed up. I wouldn't know how it would transfer over to a civilian job though.'

'Well, what do you do on the ship?'

'Maintain all the systems, mostly. Communications, weapons, navigation, that kind of thing.'

'I'm sure you would be able to find something if you had to.'

Harley felt him tense beside her, and his hand stopped moving against her arm. 'I hope it never comes to that.' His voice sounded so flat, dismissive. Had he never thought of the possibility before? Was it not an option?

She polished off the remainder of her glass of wine. 'You don't think it would be an option?'

'Not by choice.'

Harley straightened. She couldn't ignore the weight settling in her stomach, or the ache in her chest. 'Well, what if something happened?'

'Like what?'

There was something in his tone that told her she should forget that line of thought, but how could she? She'd fallen in love with Joey and she was pretty sure he was at least on his way there, too—unless she'd read the signs all wrong. Unless the way he looked at her when he thought she couldn't see him was all in her imagination. Unless the gentle, loving way he touched her and made love to her was all in her head. She knew she could fall hard for a guy. That she could feel so much more for him than he might ever feel for her. But she'd thought Joey was different. Why else would he have taken her away for the week? On a trip where they would spend every moment together? Why else would he pretend he could ride a horse just so they could have that romantic memory of a beachside sunset ride together?

'What could happen to make me think leaving the navy would be a good option?' he said, his voice firm.

Harley swallowed. 'I don't know,' she muttered, a burn starting at the back of her eyes. 'What if you found a reason to stay?'

'Like?'

'Like ... us.'

He stared at her. It was still too dark to read his expression properly, but she didn't need to. She could feel the tension between them. She could feel her heart breaking a little with every second he didn't respond.

Finally, he spoke. 'Do you know what you're asking me to do?'

'I'm just putting the idea out there,' she said, moving to the edge of the seat, turning to face him better. She reached for his hands and squeezed them, but he didn't squeeze back. He didn't move at all. 'Joey, I know it sounds bad, but is it? Jobs are never permanent—'

'It's not just a job, Harley. It's my fucking life.'

He rose to his feet and began pacing the veranda in front of her. Her body instantly missed his closeness and her heart ached to tell him to forget she'd said anything, to wish away the distance and the pain. But what was said could not be taken back. Eventually, they would have to face the facts, and the fact was that, in a few short days, he would be heading back out to sea for God knows how long and she would be left behind wondering if he was ever coming back.

'You are asking me to give up my life. Not just what I'm good at, or what I know, or what I'm qualified to do. My *life*, Harley.' He stopped pacing and slapped his hand against his chest. 'You know why I've got that tattoo? It's because I accepted long ago that this is what I would be doing. Forever. I belong in the navy, Harley. It's my anchor. It's what holds me together and keeps me grounded. It's my home. I can't throw it all aside like it's nothing. You can't expect me to.'

Her tears rolled unhindered down her cheeks. She didn't bother with trying to stop them. 'I'm not expecting you to. I'm just asking if it's an option.'

'It's not.'

'How do you know?'

'Would you quit your job, Harley? Would you change your life—for *us* ?'

Her body heaved with a sob, despite trying to hold herself together. The truth was, she would. In a heartbeat. If it meant she could spend every morning waking up with him by her side, she would do anything. But it all meant nothing if they weren't on the same page. The very thought that they might not be was like being stabbed in the gut.

'I might not have a job to go back to,' she managed through sobs. 'Okay? I might be losing all that. I might not have a choice.'

'But I do.' His words only drove the dagger in further.

'Even if I did, I would. I'd leave it all for us.'

He rubbed his hands over his face. 'It's not the same, Harley. You can't expect me to make the same choice.'

'Why? Because I'm not worth it?'

His hands dropped from his face and she caught a glimpse of regret in the tiny bit of light that shone on his face. 'Harley—'

'Because we're not on the same page? Because you thought a week away together would be a good way to pass the time and have a little fun in the process?'

'Fuck, Harley, that's not—'

'Because you don't love me the way I love you?'

The tears came freely now, and it felt like her heart was being ripped out of her chest. But better now than when she was in even deeper—if that was at all possible. There was no way of getting out of it without a broken heart. He took a step towards her and she rose to her feet, squeezing between him and the porch swing to put some distance between them. What was she doing? She'd known going away for a week would likely be a bad idea. And look at her now—just when she'd thought it could have been different. That he was different. That maybe, just maybe, she'd found her forever.

Well, she's the fool. His forever was his job.

'Harley, wait.'

'What's the point, Joey?' The tears still flowed, and she felt weary. She'd known their time would come to an end, that he'd go back to work and she'd be left behind. So why did it hurt so much? 'I can't expect you to stay.' Something had changed in his expression, but he still didn't deny it. It was still very much the truth. 'And you can't expect me to wait.'

'Harley—'

But it was too late. She went through the front door, letting it close itself, and beelined to the bathroom, locking the door behind her for the first time that trip. The tears came with no restraint then, and her sobs racked her body relentlessly. With every minute passing, she worked on building the wall around her heart again, knowing that her efforts were probably futile.

She pressed her palms against her eyes, trying to scrub away the memories of the way he'd kissed her, touched her. And the way she'd said she loved him and he hadn't said it back.

Chapter 11

Joey sat on the edge of the bed, his head resting in his hands. How had things escalated so quickly? He'd seen how hurt she was over him saying he couldn't choose her over his lifestyle. Truth was, he wanted both. He wanted to still be a sailor, doing what he loved, and he wanted Harley. But he couldn't have the best of both worlds. It was the age-old dispute he'd heard play out for anyone on his ship who'd ever been in a relationship.

He was a fool to think it might have been different for him. To think that Harley wasn't the kind of woman to make him choose.

You can't expect me to wait.

Her words still rang in his ears. He'd tried so hard not to think about it—not to worry about what would happen when he inevitably had to return to work. He'd thought that if he just ignored it and lived in the moment that *maybe* the problem might just go away. *Maybe* they would get stuck in time and be left to live their lives in this little cabin on the beautiful beachside where magic happened and they never had to worry about any damn thing happening back home. *Maybe* something would happen and the decision would be made for them. *Maybe* they wouldn't have to have a fight over something they didn't have to worry about yet.

But maybes were full of shit.

And Joey had been so determined that, if she asked, he might actually consider it as an option. But then she'd asked, and his instincts kicked into gear. He'd become so hellbent that it was never an option, that she was asking too much, that she was too much like every other woman he'd heard about that he hadn't realised what he was ultimately asking of her.

She'd said she would do anything for him—for them. She'd said she loved him. And it was at that moment that he'd snapped back to his senses. That he'd realised he hadn't imagined it all between them. That he'd made the right choice in coming back for her. But where did that leave them? He still couldn't just throw the towel in on his job. It wasn't just about him. He was in a position of leadership. He had people who relied on him to get things done. And others relied on his stories to get them through the tough months. He wished the decision were easier. He wished that he could go to bed every night with her in his arms and wake up with her lips on his like he had the last few days. But wishes didn't come true, and magic didn't happen in Margaret River—or anywhere, for that matter.

They only had three more nights together—if Harley still wanted to spend them with him. He couldn't let this fight fester and be their ruin. He had come back to win Harley over and, damn it, that's what he was going to do. When he'd started to wonder if she'd somehow already packed her bags and left, the bathroom door unlocked and slowly opened. He lowered his hands and looked up as she came into view. She paused once she saw him there, her lips pressed together in a tight line.

'Oh,' she said, as though disappointed to see him there.

His heart caught in his throat at her pale skin, her swollen, bloodshot eyes. Her tear-stained cheeks. He'd caused that. He'd hurt her. The very thing he'd wanted to avoid at all costs.

'I don't deserve you,' he whispered, rising to his feet. Her lips quivered and she took in a shaky breath, folding her arms over her chest. He shook his head, fighting his own threatening tears as he slowly closed the distance between them.

'Joey—'

'Please, Harley,' he said, knowing that he couldn't say what he really needed to if she said anything first. 'I don't. I don't deserve you. You're too good for me. Too pure.' She scoffed, and he lifted a hand to cup her chin, urging her to focus on him. 'I shouldn't have come back like this. I shouldn't have expected that a week would be enough time to figure this out. I shouldn't have thought that any part of this would be fair to you. I shouldn't want you.' He wiped a stray tear away from her cheek and saw her swallow. 'But I do. And I will never stop wanting you.'

'I shouldn't have asked—'

'No, you had a right to ask. It's your future, too. And no, I can't see it being an option right now, but it doesn't mean it'll always be that way. We need time to figure out what we can be and how we can do it, and I can't cut off my ties until we know.'

'B—but I thought it was obvious what we are,' she stammered. 'Isn't this something special? Tell me I'm not imagining it.'

He swallowed, his heart feeling both full and as though it was being torn to shreds. 'You're not imagining it. None of it. It's real, and I know it is. It's just that me leaving my work is a huge change. I would be leaving a world I know for a world I don't. Right now, I have security and a future in my career. I won't have any of that if I leave. I have to think logically.'

She dropped her gaze and let out a sigh. 'I know.'

He nudged her chin upwards with his fingers and wiped another tear from her cheek. 'I overreacted, and I'm sorry. I love you, Harley. Nothing will change that. You're my girl.'

She let out another sob and threw herself into his arms. He held her tightly, silently vowing never to let go of her if he could possibly avoid it. And before long, he was kissing her, and she was kissing him with a new fervour and passion. A kind that he'd never known was possible. Their clothes became a very distant memory and, in what seemed like a few moments too long, she was on top of him, lowering herself until he filled her completely. They moved urgently and longingly, the world around them disappearing until it was just him and Harley and the love they shared—their bodies moving as one, their breaths mingling, reaching their peak together. And as they roared over the edge, he realised how bittersweet it really was. That the woman he loved would no longer be able to share his bed after a few short nights. And the day that he was set to return to work was one hell of a bitch overshadowing every sweet memory he was trying to create.

***

They'd wasted no time over their last few days and nights together. They'd made love as much as humanly possible, barely leaving the bed if they could avoid it. The looming deadline was a topic that was no longer talked about, even though they both knew it was there. Even if it tore at Harley's heart more and more with every passing moment.

So as she curled into him after they'd made love one final time, listening to the rhythm of his heart as it beat steadily against her ear, she couldn't help but feel the ache in her chest, despite the fact they now had at least a semblance of a plan. They'd talk as much as they could. For now, he'd go back to work. He'd come see her as often as he could, but even that would never be enough. Harley wondered if they would ever really work it out or if they were just delaying the inevitable. But to hell if they were. The thought of saying goodbye to Joey for good was much more heartbreaking than the knowledge that she would see him again *someday*. She didn't know when, and she didn't know for how long, but she would see him again. And that could at least get her through each day.

The early morning sun started to filter in through the window, which meant their time together was steadily coming to an end. Oh, how she wished that she could stop time—that things could be simpler. That impossible decisions never had to be made. But she was only human, and nothing ever seemed to work in her favour. So she just had to suck it up and do her best to manage the cards she'd been dealt.

'Promise you won't go running to that dick next door?'

Harley couldn't help but laugh at the absurdity of his question, but when she glanced up at him, his expression was serious. 'Joey, you know I won't. There's only you, remember? I'm not going to run off with some other guy. Especially not him.'

'But what if—what if you get lonely?'

'I will be lonely.' She sat up, and he followed suit. 'Of course I'll be lonely. I will be unless you're here. But I'm yours. I was never his. Not really. And besides, he moved months ago.' She caught his eyes and tried her best to make sure he got the message. 'I'm yours. No one else's. Yours.'

He lifted her hand to his lips, his gentle kiss sending a flutter to her core.

Would she ever get used to his kisses, his touch? 'Promise?' His eyebrow rose and the look in his eyes darkened, sending a tingle through her whole body.

'Promise,' she said. 'Promise you won't forget me?'

'I could never forget you.'

He pulled her close and kissed her then, his lips firm yet gentle. She poured her everything into that kiss, memorising his taste, his scent, his touch. She didn't want to forget a single thing about Joey if the distance turned out to be for a longer period than she'd hoped. They broke the kiss and she snuggled back under his arm again, breathing him in.

'When do you think you'll be back again?' Without intending to, she held her breath, waiting for his answer.

'I don't know. A few months, maybe. I can apply for leave, but it doesn't mean it'll be approved.'

Harley pouted. Even a few months sounded like an agonisingly long stretch. She remembered Andie telling her how the days seemed to drag on whenever she was away from Tay. Would it be like that for her? How could she survive months of that? She frowned as his earlier question caught up to her again.

'Why were you worried I'd run off with someone else?' she asked, looking up at him.

He exhaled, long and slow, and focused on a point on her arm where his fingers traced soothing patterns. 'My pop dying wasn't the only reason I joined the navy.' She swallowed, waiting for him to continue. She'd thought there was more to the story when he'd mentioned it last time, but he hadn't said it, and she hadn't pushed it. 'I was hurt. By a girl. We'd been dating in our last year of school. You know how I said I tried a summer session?' She nodded. He let out another long breath. 'I thought I'd give it a go, just in case things got serious with her. And I thought it was. I wanted to join the navy, sure, and I thought she was supportive of it, but I held off to see where things could go. After Pop died, I went to her and—and found her with some other guy.'

'So there was nothing holding you back.'

He nodded slowly. It all made sense now. The way he reacted when she asked him if staying was an option. The way the navy had become such a huge part of his life. His hopes that she wouldn't do what his ex had done to him so many years ago.

'I haven't really been with anyone since then, Harley.'

'In what, ten years?' He nodded. 'Oh come on, I'm not sure I believe that.' A man as handsome and kind as Joey? Surely not. She could imagine women falling over him every which way. But there was something very serious in the way he looked at her. He wasn't joking around. 'Really?'

'I might talk a lot of shit, and there's been the occasional woman I've flirted with, but no. Not like this. I didn't want anything to happen unless I was serious about it. And I am. I'm serious about you, Harley.'

'I'm serious about you, too.'

Her heart felt like it expanded in her chest as she stared into his eyes, but at the same time, it hurt. God, she wanted this. All of it. She wanted to wake up every morning next to Joey, see his smile, hear his laughter. His jokes. No one could make her smile the way he did. But she couldn't have it all. At least, not yet. For now, she had to make do with what she could have. Which wasn't much, in the grand scheme of things. He broke eye contact when his alarm went off. Her heart dropped, knowing that meant they'd run out of time.

'So this is it, then?'

He brushed his thumb across her cheek, wiping away the tears she hadn't even realised had started. 'For now. But I'll be back, as soon as I can. And I'll call every chance I get.'

'And when you can't?' Her voice was shaky, and her body shook as he cupped her face in his hands.

'Then I'll write. And I'll deliver it personally.'

He pulled her close and covered her mouth with his. She gripped him wherever she could, trying to get as much of him as she could in their final moments before he left again. Her body ached for more of him, and her heart broke as he pulled away to gather his things. She tried her best to hold herself together, to be strong, but it was harder than she'd thought it would be. How was it possible that one week could have changed so much? She followed him to the door, biting into her lip to stop it from quivering. He opened the door and turned back to her, pulling her into his arms again and kissing her as if it were the last time they'd kiss. A part of her reminded herself that it might very well be the last time. She'd heard that, more often than not, distance did not make the heart grow fonder, and she desperately hoped that wouldn't be the case with them.

'See you soon, beautiful,' he said, giving her one more squeeze.

'See you soon.'

The words were so choked she wasn't sure they'd come out clearly. Joey flashed the smile that sent her stomach flipping and closed the door behind him. She waited a minute, hoping, praying, that maybe he might just come back through those doors and it had all been a misunderstanding. That he wasn't going anywhere. But with every passing moment, her knees grew weaker and the sobs took over, loneliness swamping her and the doubts creeping in.

Had he even been there at all?

Chapter 12

It was hard to believe a few weeks had passed since Joey left. It felt a heck of a lot longer than that. Harley was tired, to put it simply. She struggled to sleep with him gone, waiting for him to call—which could be at any time. The hours passed slowly and at the end of each day, she felt like she hadn't really achieved much. Every moment seemed hard. She hadn't been able to dive headfirst into work either, since there'd been no progress on the break-in and no clear indication of what Jannette was wanting to do. Andie and Libby had tried their best to help keep her mind off things, but the reality of her situation was that she was screwed.

She was in love with a guy she didn't get to see and hardly got to speak to, she may not have a job soon, and she really was starting to question, well, everything. It was just her and her new best pal, Fleur the ficus.

'What do you think, Fleur? Am I going mad?' She shoved another spoonful of ice cream into her mouth—one of the few foods she felt like. Fleur didn't answer. She never did. 'I am, aren't I? Did I imagine the whole thing?'

Still more silence. But Fleur's very presence showed that Joey had been there and she hadn't imagined that part at least. He had bought the plant for her, after all. And the necklace. She fingered the pendant around her neck and stared down at the last text she'd received from him a few days earlier. *Love you, beautiful.*

'Love you too, Joey,' she said, shoving another scoop into her mouth. How the hell was she supposed to manage months on end when she was a total mess after just a few weeks?

She heard a knock at the door and her heart leapt into her throat. Could it be him? She stared at the door as the jangle of keys sounded on the other side and the doorknob turned. No. It couldn't be. He didn't have a key. Only one other person had a key.

Erin swung the door open and let herself in, her face scrunching at the sight that met her. 'What the hell happened here?'

'Erin,' Harley managed through her mouthful. 'What are you doing here?'

Erin lugged a few grocery bags in through the door and plopped them on the kitchen bench. 'Thought you might need some company.'

'Fleur and I are getting on just fine,' Harley said. It was a poor attempt at humour and did nothing to ease her mood.

Her sister stopped unpacking the bags and looked up at her. 'Ah, Fleur?' Harley pointed to the plant in the corner. 'Oh. You named it. Har, when was the last time you opened the windows and let some air—and sunlight—in here?'

Harley bit into another mouthful. 'What are you saying?'

'You look miserable and'—her nose crinkled—'smell ... miserable.'

'Way to make me feel better,' Harley sulked. Erin ignored her, setting to work on opening the blinds and windows to air out Harley's little unit. Harley squinted at the bright, unwanted light pouring in through the windows.

'How often are you showering?'

'Ah, every day. I'm not a grub, Erin.'

'I'm just checking you're looking after yourself.' Erin flopped onto the couch next to Harley and took the tub of ice cream out of her hands, taking a scoop for herself.

'Thanks, but—'

'Yeah, but you're a big girl, yada yada.' Erin waved a hand dismissively at her as she took another scoop of Harley's ice cream. 'You're moping, Har.'

Harley shrugged, sinking into the couch. 'Got nothing else to do.'

Erin put the tub on the coffee table and placed a hand on Harley's leg. 'Still no news on work?'

'Nope.'

'It's been almost a month, hasn't it?'

'Your point?'

Erin grimaced. 'Well, I mean, if there's no news yet, maybe it's not going to be good.'

'You think I'll have to look for another job?'

'Don't you? I'm just putting it out there. You can't spend all your time waiting around for people to sort their shit out. It's not healthy.'

'You mean Joey.' Harley had spent many nights spilling everything to Erin, so her sister knew it all. Normally, she would have gone to Andie, but it just didn't seem right going to Joey's sister to mope.

'I mean Jannette. Joey, he—that's different. He can't really change things without changing *everything*. But Jannette...'

'I should talk to her, right?'

Erin nodded, as Harley knew she would. 'You need to know whether or not you should be applying for other jobs.'

Harley sighed. Her sister was right—as usual. As much as work was one of the last things on Harley's mind, she knew that she couldn't slum it at home forever. Eventually, her savings would run out and she'd have to face the hard reality of being broke and jobless. Her phone started ringing and she reached for it, her heart racing at the thought it might be Joey, but it was Andie. She let it ring out. She'd call her back later.

'I just don't know what I'd do, Erin,' Harley said, twirling her phone in her hand. 'What if I do have to find another job? What else could I do? I've been a seamstress my whole career.'

'There are other seamstress jobs out there.'

Harley shot a look at her sister. 'Yeah, but not bridal ones. The next bridal shop is on the other side of town. That's too far to go every morning.'

Erin shook her head enthusiastically. 'No, it's not. There's one way up the other end of the same street as *Bride and Beau*.'

Harley pulled her brows together as her phone rang again. Andie. Again. 'Ah, no, there's not. Ours is the only one this side.'

The phone rang out. 'There is. I drove past it on my way here.' Erin plucked her phone out of her pocket and typed something out. Then she showed the screen to Harley. Sure enough, another bridal shop was listed on the map up the other end of the street.

'Weird,' Harley said, taking the phone from her sister's hand. 'I've never seen it there before.'

'I haven't either. They must have opened in the last few weeks.'

Harley pursed her lips as she handed Erin's phone back. A new bridal shop on the *same street* as *Bride and Beau?* It seemed odd, in her opinion. But maybe they thought it was a good business district. She wondered if that was going to affect Jannette's decision to reopen or not. Harley's phone rang again—Andie—and her heart skipped a beat when the thought that maybe something had happened to Joey popped into her head. She looked at her sister.

'I should probably get this. Andie doesn't usually keep ringing unless it's important.'

'Go ahead,' Erin said, waving a hand at her. 'I'll finish putting the groceries away.'

She waited until Erin was closer to the kitchen before answering. 'Hey, Andie. Everything okay?'

'Why the hell weren't you answering?' Andie sounded stressed.

Harley's heart raced in her chest. 'What if it was an emergency?'

'Is it?'

'No. Well, I don't know. Maybe.' The line went silent on the other end.

'Andie?'

She heard Andie sigh before speaking slowly. 'Jannette wants us to come to the shop. Today. Now, actually.'

'For ... work?'

'I don't think so.' Andie's voice was solemn, and Harley knew that her fears must be coming true.

'I'll be right there.'

***

Harley walked through the same door she'd passed through almost every day of her working life and found nothing she recognised. The dress racks were empty and only the skeleton of what the shop once was remained. Her stomach twisted in knots. Was this it? Was this the end of working for Jannette?

She looked at Andie who had just come in as well. Andie shrugged. She obviously knew about as much as

Harley did. They both walked out to the bridal room—also empty—and found Jannette in the office at the back. Harley tapped on the office door and Jannette looked up. She looked pale and stressed and as though she hadn't eaten enough for a while.

'Oh, girls, thanks for coming in.'

'What's going on, Jannette?' Andie asked hesitantly.

Jannette let out a long sigh. 'Well, as you've probably guessed, we've closed for good.'

A weight dropped in Harley's stomach. 'The break-in?'

Jannette shook her head. 'Still don't know who did it. And it might not have been a targeted attack, but'—she rubbed her forehead—'I'm tired. Trying to keep this place up and running and profitable—it's exhausting. And now my brother has injured himself on the farm and he has asked if I can help out for a while. I don't know how long that will be for.'

'But you know that Harley and I can keep things going,' Andie said, clearly as baffled as Harley, even though she was sure they'd both known this was coming.

'I do. But I couldn't, in good conscience, do that to you. And I have no idea if or when I would be coming back. I've been thinking about closing for a while and, well, you girls were the reason why I didn't. But I think—I think the break-in was the determining factor. The last straw, so to speak.' She thrust an envelope out towards each of them. 'I wanted to give you this in person. It's your severance package. I know it's not the same as a job, but what's done is done. I can't express how grateful I am for the two of you and I will miss you both. A lot.'

Harley swiped at her eyes. She'd told herself she wouldn't be emotional if she ended up without a job, but she'd been a hell of a lot more emotional over the past month than she'd been in her life.

'We'll miss you, Jannette,' she said, pulling Jannette and Andie into a group hug. The three sniffed and hugged for a moment longer before Jannette pulled away.

'I thought we'd have a send-off for this old girl,' Jannette said, presenting a bottle of champagne and three glasses. 'If it wasn't for *Bride and Beau,* I wouldn't have met either of you. And I think my life has been better off because of it.' Jannette poured a generous amount of champagne into each of the glasses and raised hers. 'To new beginnings.'

Chapter 13

'Wow.'

'Wow,' Harley repeated, focusing on her best friend after they'd said goodbye to Jannette and the shop.

'Didn't see that coming,' Andie said, letting out a long breath.

'Really?' Harley had. Well, not the finer details, but in the broad spectrum, she kind of had.

'Well, I mean, I'd thought it might be a possibility, but I didn't think it would be like *this.*' Andie brushed her hair away from her face, and Harley saw something she hadn't seen before. A ring. Or more specifically, a diamond ring. She snatched at Andie's hand and looked at it, letting out a low whistle. Expensive.

'Seriously, Andie?' Andie's cheeks went red and she bit into her lip. Harley squeezed her hand. 'When? And why wasn't *that* the first thing you said on the phone?'

'Tay proposed last night, and I was just about to come over to tell you when Jannette called.' Andie grimaced.

'I didn't think it would be ... appropriate ... to be all excited while Jannette's practically having a breakdown.'

'Are you kidding me? Babe, you're freaking *engaged* ! She would have been happy for you. Now, tell me all the details.' She looped her arm through Andie's and they strolled up the street.

'Well, remember that vineyard in Darlington?'

'Your dream venue?' Andie had chosen that vineyard as her future wedding venue when she was a kid, so of course Harley knew the one.

Andie nodded. 'He took me there last night and we took a stroll through the vines, just like we did at Libby's wedding. He did the whole pretending-to-tie-his-shoelace thing and—' Andie shrugged, her smile unhindered.

Harley squealed. 'And you said yes!'

'I said yes.'

She squeezed Andie's arm as they walked. 'God, I'm so happy for you. When's the wedding?' Andie mumbled something that sounded to Harley like it was in no time at all, and Harley blinked. 'Come again?'

'Six weeks.'

'*Six weeks?* Are you crazy?'

Andie laughed. 'Maybe. But we didn't want to wait, and there was an opening and, well, you know the drill.'

'Mmm, I know you've had every part of your wedding planned out since you were a little girl, so if anyone can plan a wedding in six weeks, it's you. Does—does Joey know?'

Andie's eyes glimmered with excitement. Harley knew that Andie loved the fact that her and Joey were together now. She really hoped it would stay that way. What would happen if things didn't work out with him? Could Harley and Andie still be friends? Surely they could. They were friends long before she'd ever met Joey. But then, she was also sure she wouldn't be able to hang out with Andie without thinking about her brother.

'Apparently Joey knew before I did,' Andie said, her eyebrow raised. 'Tay asked him for his blessing.'

'How romantic.' Harley pulled out her phone and dialled a number.

'Who are you calling?'

'Libby.'

'Why?'

'Well, if you're getting married in six weeks, we're going to need a dress. And I know just the place.'

***

Joey smiled at the message with the wedding details on his phone. Andie was getting married. About bloody time. He hadn't been surprised when Tay contacted him to ask for his blessing to marry Andie and to tell him the date—now only three weeks away—so he could put in leave. If he was being honest, he was wondering when they were going to seal the deal. Those two were perfect for each other. But a six-week engagement? Well, if anyone could organise a wedding in record time, it was his sister. In fact, by the sounds of it, Andie had done a pretty good job of doing just that, with Harley and Libby's help. Everything had supposedly been organised with three weeks to spare. It was going to be a small, intimate gathering, but still. That was one hell of a feat. Harley had sounded excited that he'd be coming back for the wedding, but again, he wouldn't be able to stay for more than a week. And after *that* trip back, he wasn't sure how long it would be before the next.

He hadn't realised how much he could truly miss her. Sure, he'd missed her before, but this—this was something else. This had every second feeling like minutes, and every minute feeling like hours, and every hour feeling like days. Don't even get him started on how the days felt. And after every call and every time he stared at the pictures on his phone of the two of them together at Margaret River, the thought of being away from her for so long was getting to him.

He missed her with every fibre of his being. He missed feeling her body against his, feeling her touch, her kisses, the smell of her sweet perfume and gentle fragrance of her shampoo. And yet, as much as he wanted to be with her, he still had responsibilities on the ship. That hadn't changed.

He wished it could have been different. It had broken his heart leaving her behind again. Especially how she'd tried to be so strong about it. He hadn't wanted anything more than he'd wanted to fly back through her door and take her in his arms, promising her he'd never leave her again—not for a second. But he couldn't. Not yet. And he'd tried to figure out when and if he'd ever be able to promise her that. And still he had nothing.

Distance sucked.

'Hey, Gray.' Joey glanced up at Ryan, who jerked his head, indicating for Joey to follow him. 'Officers' meeting. Captain wants to talk to us.'

Joey tucked his phone away and followed his friend. Officers' meetings weren't uncommon, but they were usually scheduled. This was not. He followed Ryan into the meeting room and looked around. If he calculated correctly, it looked as though every officer on the ship was in there.

'Must be serious,' Ryan muttered, standing off to the side.

Joey nodded, glancing up at the captain. His expression was solemn and, as Ryan pointed out, it did look serious. There was a kind of tension in the room. Uncertainty. Worry. He wasn't sure what else. The captain checked that everyone was there, then began.

'There's no easy way to say this, so I'm just going to say it,' the captain said. Joey frowned. What could *possibly* be that serious? 'The HMAS *Mallee* is being decommissioned.'

The room was silent, and Joey's heart dropped to his stomach. His ship was being decommissioned? No, he must have heard incorrectly. He scanned the room around him. Every person in the room had the same look that he was sure he had on his face. Considering most of them had spent their entire navy careers on the HMAS *Mallee,* it was pretty big news to take in. This ship was their home, their life. And if it was being decommissioned ... well, then their home was being taken away from them.

'As you all know,' the captain continued, 'this old girl has been in service a long time, and I know each and every one of you feel the same way about her as I do.'

He paused to take a long, steadying breath. Joey's throat burned. He glanced at his friend. Ryan's jaw was tense, his brow creased. So he'd heard right. It really was being decommissioned.

'Eventually, the time comes around for every ship. Unfortunately, this time, it's ours. She will be decommissioned in a month and, with it, we have all been given a rare opportunity to make a decision of our own. You may choose to put in a transfer to another ship, or discharge at the same time as the decommission—go down with the ship, so to speak.' The captain paused, looking around the room. His eyes seemed to shimmer, a sadness filling them. 'I've been on this ship for my entire career and I'm close enough to retiring to not want to start again somewhere else. As the captain of the HMAS *Mallee*, I will be going down with my ship. But I cannot make your decision for you. Each and every one of your decisions is personal and will depend on your personal choices and your career aspirations.'

The captain continued talking, but Joey heard none of it. His ship was going down. The ship that had been his home since he'd left training. He scanned the room again. All these people had become his family. He didn't necessarily like or get along with every single one of them, but they were family, nonetheless. And in a month's time, they would all be separated. Some might transfer to the same ships. Others might still see each other if they discharged. But in essence, his family was breaking up.

His heart pounded in his chest as he wondered what the hell he was going to do. Sailing is what he knew—what he was good at. It was his anchor, as he'd told Harley. But he still couldn't imagine ever transferring to another ship and trying to fit in with another crew. When he'd thought of his career in the future, it was there on the HMAS *Mallee* with the people around him now. And while everyone else had a month to decide, he only had three weeks. By the time he got back from Andie's wedding, his ship would already have gone down. He would be returning to a ship that wasn't his home, to people who weren't his family.

And that was a decision he'd never thought he'd ever have to make.

Chapter 14

Harley had never been so excited—and nervous—in her life.

Her best friend was getting married to the perfect man for her. And Harley would see Joey again after two long, agonising months. It felt like it had been years since she'd last seen him—touched him—and the butterflies were stirring in her stomach at the thought she would finally get to see him again. Would it be the same? Would they still feel as strongly for each other as they did when she saw him last?

Over their time apart, she'd begun to suspect that she'd imagined a lot of it and that maybe her memories were a lot more romanticised than what had actually happened. The doubts had crept in, implanting the idea in her mind that maybe their efforts were pointless. Sure, they'd talked as much as they could over the past couple of months, but few of those conversations seemed to be private and longer than just a few minutes. And he always seemed distracted, especially over the last few weeks.

They'd planned to figure something out, yet nothing had changed, and it didn't look as though it would anytime soon. He was still committed to his job, and Harley was still left behind waiting for the next time she'd see or hear from him again. Erin had told her she needed to get out of her head—that she thought too much. She'd told Harley to wait it out as long as she could. Things took time, and maybe this was one of those things.

Harley hoped she was right.

She hoped that Joey would still feel the same for her as she did for him. And soon she would find out.

From what she'd managed to gather, Joey had come in the night before and, since Andie and Tay were practising tradition, she'd had to spend the evening before the wedding with Andie and Libby, unable to escape to see him. She'd hoped she might have caught a glimpse of him in the morning, but she'd forgotten how busy it could be for a bride and her bridesmaids.

The three of them had just finished getting ready when Libby poured a few glasses of champagne and divvied them up between the three of them. Libby raised her glass and Andie and Harley followed suit.

'I never thought I would ever get the chance to say this, since Tay can be a real tough nut to crack,' she said, taking a deep breath, smiling excitedly at Andie. 'Cheers, Andie, for taming my brother.' She turned towards Harley next. 'And to you, Harley, for taming Andie's brother.'

The three of them laughed, Harley's cheeks heating. The thought of having her own special day like this with Joey was something that filled her dreams. She knew there was a lot more to it than that—distance being a huge contributing factor—but she wasn't going to bring that up on Andie's special day.

'Oh, can you imagine?' Libby continued, her eyes glistening with unshed tears. 'The three of us could actually be sisters!'

The thought of the three of them being sisters did sound amazing, but still. Harley didn't want to get her hopes up. 'You do know that Joey and I aren't getting married, right?'

'Not yet,' Libby squeaked, sipping her champagne. Harley thought she caught something in the glance between Libby and Andie, but she had no time to question it.

'Knock, knock.' The familiar voice made her spin on her heel as Jannette wandered over to the three of them.

Andie shrieked and raced towards her, her beautiful A-line lace and chiffon wedding gown swishing gracefully as she moved. 'You made it!'

'Of course I did,' Jannette said, pulling Harley into their embrace as well. 'I wouldn't miss it for the world. Besides, I had some news to share.'

'You're coming back to open the shop?' Harley said hopefully. She had to admit, Jannette looked a lot less stressed, her skin slightly tanned—no doubt from her farm work which Harley still couldn't believe. Who knew that beneath all the fancy dress and pretty makeup that Jannette was actually a farm kid?

'No, I'm not. But they finally found the people who broke in. It was just some kids having fun and wasn't related to any of the targeted attacks in the area.' Jannette let out a long breath.

'Well, I'm glad it wasn't targeted,' Andie said.

'Me, too,' Jannette said. 'And the way it came about wasn't ideal, but in a way, I'm a little glad it happened. I think I would have still been stuck in an endless cycle of bills and *what-if* s if I didn't have that nudge.' She turned towards Harley. 'I heard you started working for the bridal shop up the road.' Harley nodded. She had, though she hadn't wanted to broadcast it—especially to her old boss. 'Well, good. I know the owner. She's a friend of mine from way back. She'll look after you.'

They chatted for a few more moments and Jannette helped with all the finishing touches before excusing herself to join the rest of the small crowd. Soon enough, the three of them were waiting just out of sight, ready for the outdoor ceremony to start.

***

Joey wiped his sweaty palms on his pants, stuffed them into his pockets, then remembering he was at his sister's wedding, removed them and folded his hands in front of him. The tie around his throat felt unusually tight and he reached up to adjust it, beads of sweat forming on his forehead despite the cool air surrounding them.

'Everything all right over there?' Tay's best man, Connor, said. 'Some might think it's your wedding.'

Joey tried to talk, some kind of croak coming out, then cleared his throat. 'All good.'

Tay leaned around his best man, the three of them lined up near the garland. 'You look nervous enough for the both of us, Joey.'

'Well, it is my sister's wedding,' he muttered. Tay gave him a knowing smile.

Sure, it was Andie's wedding. But it was also the first time in months that he'd see Harley, and he was nervous as hell. The last few weeks had been a heck of a lot more than he'd bargained for, and he'd had to make possibly the hardest decision of his life.

He desperately hoped he'd made the right choice.

And even more so, he hoped that his connection with Harley was everything he remembered it to be—if not more. Saying the distance between them had been hard would be a huge understatement. He just hoped it hadn't taken its toll. That Harley hadn't decided she couldn't do this anymore.

Harley was the love of his life. And living without her would be something akin to living without air.

The pews in front of them were steadily filling with the small crowd that had fallen under the category of close friends and family. Among them, he saw his own parents moving towards the front row, his mum flashing him a smile as she settled into her seat. He smiled back, then felt the familiar fist in his chest as his dad made his way towards the three of them. He kept his eyes on his father, unanswered questions pushing to the forefront of his mind as the older man avoided eye contact.

His dad came to a stop in front of Tay, his hand extended and his grin wide. Proud. 'Welcome to the family, son,' he said to Tay. A pang of jealousy ripped through Joey and he hated the fact that his father still had that affect. After all these years. Despite everything.

Unable to focus on the remainder of their conversation, he clenched his fists in front of him and squeezed his eyes shut to gain control over himself. By the time he opened his eyes, his dad was standing in front of him, a look in his eyes that confused him.

'Dad,' Joey said flatly. 'Andie will be glad you made it.'

His dad's Adam's apple moved as he swallowed, his lips pressed together, though Joey thought he'd seen a slight quiver. 'You look good, Trevor.'

It lacked the criticising undertone that usually laced his father's voice whenever he spoke to him, and it made Joey wonder. 'Did you get my email?'

Between returning from Margaret River and going back to work, and with Harley and his mother's help, Joey had organised for a DNA test to be done. He'd received the results via email and had forwarded it to his father with a message. Short, succinct. Nothing fancy.

Dad. For your peace of mind. Trevor.

He hadn't been able to manage anything else. He figured the results would speak for him. Really, he wasn't sure whose peace of mind it had been for. A small part of him had hoped that he wasn't his son to justify the way he'd been treated growing up. Another part of him knew that it didn't matter either way.

He held his father's eyes now, waiting for a response, refusing to look away, even when his father looked uncomfortable under his steady gaze. But there was still something in his eyes that Joey hadn't seen before. A sadness. Regret?

Finally, his father spoke. 'I did.'

'And?'

His father swallowed again, his hands twisting together in front of him before he let them fall to his side. 'I didn't look at the file.'

Joey felt the weight drop in his stomach. Even after all these years, after wanting his mother to get a test done when he was just a child, the man was still too proud and stubborn for his own good.

'I don't need a test to tell me that you're my son.'

Joey blinked, not sure if he'd heard his dad correctly. Who was this man? The man who had never gotten close to him his whole life, using the fact he didn't think Joey was his son as an excuse ... and now this? Had he known all along and just not wanted him? Joey swallowed, then swallowed again, trying to work through the lump stuck in his throat.

'I owe you an apology,' his father continued. 'I was going through a rough patch and I laid the blame on your mother. By the time you were a teenager, I knew you couldn't be anyone else's. You were my son. You looked just as I had at your age and had the determination to go with it. But by then it was too late. The damage had been done. How could I ask forgiveness from a son I didn't deserve? You were closer to your pop, and it was probably better that way.'

Joey was only slightly aware of the hustle around them, the change in atmosphere. He was still trying to process what his dad was trying to say, and he had no time to respond.

'It wasn't that I was never proud of you, Trevor, but I was scared. Scared I'd reach out to you and you wouldn't want anything to do with me. Scared I'd lose my son. But I'd already lost you, hadn't I?'

His mind was still reeling when the celebrant came up to them and rested a hand on his father's shoulder. 'She's ready for you.'

Joey watched as his dad swiped at his eyes, gave him a weak smile, and turned to walk away. 'Dad,' he called out, the fog in his head starting to clear.

His father turned to face him, and Joey realised that the coldness he'd always seen in his eyes was not hate, but grief. He'd had to live with the thought that he'd lost his son long ago because of his own stupid actions. And he'd still been living with it long after Joey had left home.

'It's not too late.'

His father blinked, a glimmer of hope flickering in his eyes. His smile was more genuine now, and he nodded before turning away again to walk his daughter down the aisle.

It was then that Joey caught Tay and Connor staring at him. He took in a deep breath and nodded, the two men smiling at him before turning their eyes forward. And Joey's nerves returned. The bridal tune began, and then he saw her.

Harley.

Her eyes locked on his the second she saw him, and his heart pounded ferociously in his chest. It was as though the nerves disappeared and he felt like he was home again. She was so beautiful, her soft brown hair styled in gentle waves over her shoulders, her smile seeming to radiate sunshine around them, warming him from the inside out. Even her dress was beautiful. He remembered her saying it was mauve and something about tulle, but none of that meant anything to him except for the fact that she made it look about a billion times better than it was. It was a simple dress, and yet she looked like a princess.

He couldn't wipe the smile from his face as she walked down the aisle towards him, and he couldn't stop the image that formed in his mind of her doing just that, but in a white dress instead of mauve.

***

The ceremony was beautiful and passed without a hitch. Andie hadn't been kidding when she'd said that it would be small and intimate—family, mostly, and a few close friends. But even so, it was still the most beautiful wedding Harley had ever seen. Andie really did get her happily ever after, after all. Harley glanced over at Joey, his eyes on her, and couldn't help but wish that she would get hers, too. After all, Darlington Vineyard had already worked its magic on Andie and Tay. Maybe it still had some magic to spare.

Harley smiled as she recalled the way Joey had looked at her as she walked down the aisle. Seeing him there at the end and seeing the way he looked at her ... well, she'd felt like a princess. She'd felt like it was her own special day, not her best friend's. And with all the glimpses she'd caught of him watching her, his eyes burning with a fire that made her toes curl and a delicious shiver run down her spine, she wondered if he'd felt the same.

She had to wait until after the ceremony had finished and the bride and groom were whisked off for their couple photographs before she could get Joey alone. He led her between the vines, her heart pounding in her chest, and as soon as they were far enough away from the rest of the crowd, he turned towards her, pulling her into his arms and kissing her until her knees went weak. It felt the same as before—if not better. God, she'd missed him. Everything about him. And she knew, in her heart, that he wasn't back for long, but he was here *now*. And that was all that mattered.

After a while, he pulled back, just enough to rest his forehead against hers. 'Hello, beautiful.'

Her cheeks grew hot, and the fire spread through her body. Oh, what she'd give to hear him say that all the time. 'Hey,' she managed.

'I missed you.'

'I missed you, too.'

He kissed her again, tenderly this time, holding her close. For a moment, she felt as though time really had stopped. He pulled away again, lifting her hand to his lips. It still sent her stomach flipping in ways she'd never imagined possible.

'I was wondering when I might get you alone,' he said.

'Me, too,' she said, still amazed that he was here again, even if it was for his sister's wedding. 'How long are you back for?'

He hesitated, and she feared that he might have only been back for the wedding and no more. 'I wanted to talk to you about that.'

He lowered her hand, but still held it. His expression was so serious that it made her think of the worst possible conclusions. He was breaking up with her. He was going away for an indefinite amount of time—deployed, maybe, where his life might be in danger. Oh, God.

'What is it?' she whispered, mentally readying herself for the worst.

'Harley, my ship has been decommissioned.' Harley shook her head, not understanding. 'They're sinking it,' he explained. 'My ship is no longer my ship. And they—they gave us a choice.'

'What kind of choice?'

His brow creased, a sadness in his eyes. 'To transfer to another ship somewhere else.'

Meaning he wouldn't be able to come back as often—if at all. 'Oh.'

'But I don't want to go to another ship. My ship was just that—*my* ship. It was my home. Going to another wouldn't be the same.'

Her mind was still reeling from the news that he wasn't going to be so close to her anymore. 'Oh, Joey, I'm so sorry.'

He shook his head. 'I took the other option.'

She frowned. 'What other option?'

He swallowed, squeezing her hands, a smile playing at his lips. 'To go down with my ship.'

She blinked a few times, trying to figure out what kind of cryptic riddle he was giving her. 'Joey, what—'

'I've discharged, Harley. I've left with my ship. I'—he held both of her hands now, pulling them up between them—'I'm back for good.'

She wasn't sure she'd heard him right at first, but his words were there, clear as day. *I'm back for good.* 'Really?' It was barely a whisper.

'Really.'

His smile was contagious, and she couldn't help but feel the excitement welling inside her. She flung her arms around him and kissed him as he swung her around, making her feel as light as a feather. He lowered her to the ground, and she looked at him with amazement.

'But—are you sure? I thought being a sailor was your life.'

He shook his head. 'That ship was my home—had been since I started. And when they told us it was being decommissioned, I realised that it was no longer the case.' He cupped her cheek in his hand. 'You are, Harley. You're my anchor now. You're my home.'

'But what about work? What will you do?'

'Turns out Tay has a lot of contacts. He's lined me up with a job using my degree.'

She blinked back the tears, still unable to believe what she was hearing. A wave of relief washed over her. 'You really mean it?'

'I really mean it. I'm back for good. I love you, Harley, and I'm all in. So what do you say, beautiful?'

Before Harley knew what was happening, he'd dropped to one knee and held a small velvet box between them. She wasn't sure if her heart stopped beating completely or if it beat so quickly that it seemed as though it had stopped. He cracked the box open to reveal an amethyst set in a ribbon of gold and smaller diamonds, almost identical to the pendant he'd given her except in the form of a ring. Her hand reached to the pendant that hung around her neck. The pendant that had given her a bit of comfort those past weeks when she had really felt the distance between them.

'Joey,' she breathed.

'I got this when I got your pendant,' he said, a slight shake in his voice. 'I knew then that I couldn't live without you. Marry me, Harley? Be my fiancée for real? I promise I'll never leave you again.'

No words would come, so Harley simply nodded, a tear rolling down her cheek as she pulled him to his feet and flung her arms around him, kissing him with a passion she'd never thought she was capable of. He broke the kiss and removed the ring from the velvet box.

'Yes?' His eyes shimmered with that mischievous look she'd loved from the start and his eyebrow shot up.

'Yes.' It was barely a whisper, but his smile showed he'd heard it. He slipped the ring on her finger and lifted her hand to kiss it without breaking eye contact. She bit into her lip, the butterflies beating hard at her insides. Would she ever get used to the way he made her feel? She hoped not. If she could feel like this every day for the rest of her life...

'I love you, beautiful.' It seemed to have so much more meaning than any other time he'd said it and her love for him bubbled inside her.

'I love you, too. So, so much.'

They kissed again, this time not rushing. They took the time to explore each other, to make up for the months apart, and Harley's heart soared with the knowledge that she would never have to deal with an impending deadline again. That Joey was back for good. And he had really, truly come back for her.

For the first time ever, she knew what it really meant to be happy and in love. And as she stood in Joey's arms, her heart fuller than she'd ever thought possible, she sent a silent thank you to the vineyard for having just a little magic to spare.

Thanks for reading *Be My Valentine.* I hope you enjoyed it.

If you liked this book, here is my other title; **Save The Date.** Keep reading for a sneak peek.

Sign up to our newsletter romance. com.au/newsletter/ and find out about new releases, must-read series and **ebook deals** at romance.com.au.

Reviews can help readers find books, and I am grateful for all honest reviews. Thank you for taking the time to let others know what you've read, and what you thought.

Share your reading experience on:

Facebook
Instagram
romance.com.au

Bestselling Titles by Escape Publishing...

Discover another great read from Escape Publishing...
Save the Date
R.J. Groves

One dressmaker. One billionaire. Two broken hearts. How long could it last?

Darlington Vineyard is the perfect wedding venue, and Andie Gray has always made sure she had a date booked, with or without a fiance. Her dreams come true when she lands the perfect man to go with the perfect venue, but then she discovers he's not who she thought he was. All of a sudden love and fairy tales no longer make sense, leaving her questioning everything about her life...

Taylor Ballin knows what he wants, and love isn't it. He's been burned before, and it won't happen again. How was he to know that offering to pay for his sister's wedding would bring bridal seamstress Andie Gray, with her maddening allure, into his world and tear down the walls he'd built around his heart?

She's the kind of woman he's spent ten years avoiding, and he's everything her ex is. But the pull between them is unavoidable and neither of them can fight it. Perhaps a no-strings-attached kind of deal is exactly what they both need.

Or is it the one thing they should avoid?

Read on for a sneak peak of *Save the Date* by R.J. Groves.

Chapter 1

Andie couldn't tear her eyes away from the mirror.

She looked—felt—pretty. Prettier than she ever had before. Her breath caught in her throat. It felt like a chokehold. She wasn't used to these mixed feelings. She wasn't used to feeling beautiful and shattered at the same time.

Ever since she was a child, she'd dreamed about her perfect wedding at that beautiful vineyard in Darlington, with fairy lights and paper lanterns as far as the eye could see. Surrounded by flowers and loved ones. A wedding that looked as though it had just been pulled from a Disney movie. She'd always wanted it, dreamed of it. It would be perfect. Magical. She'd believed in fairy tales, and that was going to be hers.

Not anymore.

She struggled to believe in anything now.

'You 'kay, babe?' Harley said, plucking another pin from her mouth and sticking it in the side of the wedding dress.

Andie blinked at the mirror, forcing herself to breathe again, her eyes drifting down at the magnificent wedding dress she was wearing. It shouldn't affect her like this. It was just a dress, after all.

'Tell me again why I have to wear this thing?' she said, her voice shaky. She forced herself to take another deep breath before she worked herself into a panic attack.

Harley pulled the remaining pin from her mouth and stuck it in near Andie's hip. Andie cringed as the pin pierced her skin. She hoped she wouldn't bleed on the dress. For Harley's sake.

'Your measurements are closer to the model's than mine,' Harley said, frowning at the last pin she'd just stuck in. She tugged on the fabric and Andie felt like her insides were being squeezed up to her throat. 'I need to pull it in a couple more inches. I swear that girl has no hips.' Harley leaned to the side to write her notes in her book.

Andie turned a little and eyed her reflection. As beautiful as this dress was, the mermaid cut just didn't feel flattering on her. No doubt that model thrived in dresses like this. While the model was only slightly curvy and mostly skin and bones, Andie was a tad more generous in the hips and chest, her waist a little thicker.

'What's wrong with the mannequin?' Andie said, glancing up at the time. She had a ten o'clock who should be arriving any moment, and she did not intend on meeting them in a wedding dress.

'You can only do so much on a mannequin,' Harley said, rising to her feet and gathering up her work. 'And since this monster refuses to come to the fittings and insists on complaining the fit is wrong at the photo shoot, I need to make do with what I've got.' She stilled, studying Andie. 'It's never bothered you before.'

Andie swallowed. She'd tried not to let what happened affect her work. She knew it would be hard to continue working in a bridal shop after her engagement fell through. But she had to try her best. Had to keep herself distracted.

'That was before...' she muttered, feeling herself taking short, quick breaths. God, it was hard to breathe in this thing.

'Of course,' Harley said, her expression apologetic. 'I'm sorry, I didn't think. It's still recent.'

Indeed, it was. Six weeks had done nothing to ease the pain. She heard the phone ring from the front room, and Harley grimaced at her, her arms full of fabric scraps and notes.

'Do you mind getting that?' she said. 'I need to deal with all this before I forget what needs to be done.'

Andie's eyebrow lifted and she glanced down at the dress she was wearing. 'In this?'

Harley grimaced again. 'I know. I'll only be a minute. Then I'll help you get out of that thing.'

'Fine,' Andie muttered, shuffling towards the front room.

Shuffling, because that's all she could do in this damn thing. It hugged her body so tightly she worried that bigger steps would either kill her or make her burst out of the dress. And Harley had put too much work into it to damage it now. She reached the phone just in time and booked in yet another anxious bride for an appointment. She wondered why so many brides were anxious when planning the biggest day of their lives. She hadn't been anxious about her wedding at all.

Perhaps she should have been.

Writing a note next to the appointment in the book, she hung up the phone and heard the jingle as the front door opened.

Great.

Her ten o'clock was here and she was still in this damned dress.

'I won't be a moment.' She finished writing the note and glanced up.

She froze.

Had she stopped breathing again?

It was magnificent.

He was magnificent.

Broad, strong shoulders filled his suit well. She'd warrant the rest of his torso was just as solid beneath his shirt. Shoulders like that almost guaranteed it. His suit was tailored to fit and boy, did it fit him well. His strong thighs seemed to hold promises. Was that possible? And his shoes were neat, polished, squared at the toes. She lifted her gaze and felt her heart pound against her chest.

He was taller than her. If she had her highest heels on, she would only reach his shoulders. God, even his neck looked strong. He had dark brown hair that was slightly too long but neatly trimmed, a perfectly square jaw sporting trimmed stubble, and his eyes—she couldn't quite discern them. His gaze made her feel both intimidated and as though she was a specimen.

This was not her ten o'clock.

Her ten o'clock went by the name of Libby Ballin.

And he was no Libby Ballin.

***

She was like a wild deer caught in the headlights.

Her eyes were wide and round, her auburn hair tied in a neat bun at the base of her head, her fringe resting to one side. Her nose was straight, her chin pointed, her neck slender. Something stirred inside him and he banished the feeling. His eyes followed the rest of her, falling to the roundness of her breasts looking as though they might burst out of the strapless dress. Tay's gaze followed her curves, lingering at her supple hips before he realised what she was wearing.

A wedding dress.

He cleared his throat, dropping his gaze. A feeble attempt to regain control over himself. Hell, when had he ever been the kind of guy to lose control around a beautiful woman? His eyes shifted back to look at her again—still frozen in place—and he diverted his gaze once more. Obviously, the woman was here for a fitting. And therefore, was already with someone. Not that it mattered. He had neither the time nor the patience for relationships.

'I was assured we had the first appointment.'

He barely recognised his own voice. Rough. Choked. Annoyed? He sure as hell felt annoyed. He'd told Libby to get the first appointment of the day. He was short on time and needed this done and dusted as soon as possible. He didn't have time to wait until another woman finished a lengthy fitting.

Hearing no response from the woman, he glanced back. She still hadn't moved. His whole body clenched, though from annoyance or stopping himself from taking her in his arms, he wasn't entirely sure. Perhaps a bit of both.

'Does anyone work here?' he called out, a little louder to reach anyone out back.

He didn't shift his gaze from the woman, and hadn't missed her flinch when he'd called out. Curious. He took a step closer, then another. She blinked. He could see the rise and fall of her chest and he hated that each heave made him pulse below the belt.

She's unavailable.

He stopped when he reached the reception desk. 'Pretty dress,' he said, hoping it sounded casual instead of choked. 'When's the wedding?'

She blinked again, her brow creasing, something changing in her eyes. They were mysterious. A shade of green that could almost be mistaken for brown unless you were up close. He nodded, indicating the dress she was wearing. Slowly, her eyes dropped. His eyes followed, noticing her white knuckles as one hand pressed against the appointment book and the other clutched a pen.

'Oh,' she said shakily, slowly releasing the pen and lifting her gaze to meet his again. 'It's not ... mine.' His eyebrow lifted. Her cheeks reddened. 'I'm just helping Harley with some adjustments.' She laughed awkwardly. 'This is supposed to be for a photo shoot but the model refuses to come for the fittings.'

He pressed his lips together. So, the woman had found her words. Such a sweet voice.

It's not hers.

Didn't mean she was available. Not that it changed anything. He was grateful for the bench between them.

'You work here?' he said. She nodded. He let out a breath. At least they didn't have to worry about waiting for someone else to finish their fitting. But where the hell was Libby? He tapped his hand on the bench. 'I'm here for a ten o'clock.'

She squinted, her lips pursed, supple. Then she shook her head, her hair flicking against her chin as she moved. 'No, you're not. You must have the wrong place.'

The wench didn't even check her appointment book. He pressed his fingers into the bench and glanced down at the book. 'Libby Ballin, see? Ten o'clock.'

She slammed the book shut. 'Yes, but you are not Libby Ballin. I spoke to Libby Ballin and she sounded very much more feminine than you do. Now, if you'll excuse me.' She started shuffling towards the back room.

His eyes fell to her full ass, watching as she wobbled awkwardly. That dress looked rather restricting. How did anyone move in it? He didn't care. He tore his gaze away from her and took a deep controlling breath. He had to get this over with.

'Is she here?' he called after her.

She turned slightly—only her head, he noticed. 'Who?'

'Libby.'

She squinted again, pressing her lips together. 'No.'

He watched her shuffle through the curtain separating the rooms and turned back to examine the front of the store.

So, Libby was late. Damn it. She knew he had meetings all afternoon. A long five minutes must have passed before the woman wandered back out to the front room, halting when she saw him. She'd changed from the wedding dress into a black pencil skirt, black heels, and a tucked-in white satin shirt. It was clear this woman meant business.

'You're still here,' she said.

He opened his mouth to retort when the door opened and Libby came flying in ungracefully. 'Oh, God, I am so sorry,' Libby said, her breathing rushed. She glanced briefly at him and smiled. 'You made it.' Before waiting for a response, she focused back on the woman. 'I didn't realise how late I was. I haven't missed it have I?'

The woman's countenance seemed to change immediately. Appealing to the target audience, he supposed. After all, Libby was her customer. 'Of course not,' the woman said, taking Libby's coat and indicating towards the back room. 'I'm Andie.' *Andie.* 'Come this way, Miss Ballin. We keep the gowns out the back—makes it more private. This is all about you, after all. Can I get you some champagne?'

He was sure Libby blushed. 'Oh, my,' Libby said. 'Champagne. Of course I'll have a glass.'

'Just the one?' Andie said, her eyes sparkling. His teeth clenched. *This* was why he'd opted to come with Libby. He couldn't have anyone taking advantage of her and charging more than they should. Especially since he was the one paying for it. 'Are your bridesmaids joining you, Miss Ballin?'

'Please, call me Libby,' Libby said, laughing awkwardly. 'I'm sure it's not what you're used to, but I don't want to show my bridesmaids until I've made a decision. I didn't want to encumber them with telling me lies about a dress they don't like but think I like, you know?'

Encumber? Hell, even being in a classier environment seemed to make Libby sound more sophisticated.

'I understand,' Andie said, ushering her towards the back room. Her voice was silky smooth. Tay didn't trust her. He followed. 'Well, don't you worry. We will find the perfect gown for your day.'

Andie turned towards him once Libby was safely through the curtain. 'Most men aren't allowed in the back room,' she said defiantly.

He shrugged his suit jacket off and draped it over her arm—the one holding Libby's coat—and flashed her a smile. She glared at him. 'I'm not most men.'

He made a move for the back room, but she stepped between him and the curtain. Her eyes shot daggers. He could smell her, since there was little space between them. Something sweet, light, but not overpowering—her perfume—and something womanly, intoxicating. Her. He could feel the warmth of her body and felt it shoot to his core.

'I don't know who you are—' she started.

'I'm the money,' he said, matter-of-factly. She squinted. He made another move for the curtain, but she stepped in front of him again. Her body was practically pressed against his.

'It's bad luck for you to see the wedding dress before the day.'

Clearly, she was clutching at straws. Despite barely coming to his shoulders, she looked up at him defiantly, her jaw set. It was ... cute. Alluring. Damn it. 'I'll take my chances.' She didn't budge. He bent lower, bringing his face closer to hers. 'Move aside, *Andie,* unless you would like us to take our business elsewhere.'

Leaning that close was a bad idea. He hadn't realised just how intoxicating she was until it was too late. He dropped his gaze to her lips and wondered if she tasted as sweet as she smelled. Her mouth twitched. Her lips were set in a fine line. He'd like to kiss that stubbornness away. She swallowed, then stepped aside, pulling the curtain back for him.

He straightened, taking a deep breath to steady himself. 'Good choice,' he said. 'I'll have some of that champagne, too. Can't let Libby have all the fun.'

She hesitated, her eyes following him as he moved to sit himself in one of the plush chairs. He could feel her gaze on his back and wondered if he should be worried that she might start throwing real daggers at him.

Thanks for reading this sample of *Save the Date* by R.J. Groves.

www.ingramcontent.com/pod-product-compliance
Lightning Source LLC
Chambersburg PA
CBHW011556010726
47495CB00010B/2808